STARTUP•LOVE

" *We stood idly and silently, gazing*
with eyes that dreamed and did not see "

ROMAN SAVIN

STARTUP
DOT
LOVE

AN IT-NOVEL ABOUT
LOVE, STARTUPS
AND
THE GOLDEN GATE BRIDGE

—

www.qatutor.com

ISBN: 978-1-7354095-1-1

This is a work of fiction. Names, characters, businesses, places, events, locales, and incidents are either the products of the author's imagination or used in a fictitious manner. Any resemblance to actual persons, living or dead, or actual events is purely coincidental.

Author and publisher:
Roman Savin (roman@qatutor.com).

First printing edition 2020.

Publisher's website: www.qatutor.com.

Printed in the United States of America.

IN LOVING MEMORY OF
NIKITA TOULINOV

MANY THANKS TO

Alex Khatilov, Alyona Kunilova, Amy Paschal, Anitha Vaidyanathan, Anna Efimenko, Antony Gradsky, Arina Latysh, Cameron Bigger, C.H., Dan Williams, Daniel Kionka, Daniel Trefts, Daria Nikitina, Dina Sabitova, E.M., Igor Nikolaev, James Kellas, J.K., Jessica Novak, John Canicosa, Juan Francisco Garrido, Konstantin Latysh, Marina Latysh, Marina Osmolovskaya, Mark Williams, Maximilian Latysh, Nikita Toulinov, Pamela Hennessy, Peter Kvitek, Peter Petrovich, P.T., Prashant Nedungadi, Ruslan Khaydarov, Sal Giambanco, Sergei Korsun, Shmagi Gulbani, S.C., Tanya Tkacheva, Vadim Kotlyar, Vladimir Osmolovsky, Zoya Savenkova.

For Hamlet,
greatness means
willingness
to fight
for reasons
as thin
as an eggshell.

— Peter Thiel,
Zero to One: Notes on Start Ups,
or How to Build the Future.

STARTUP•LOVE

Prologue

N OT LONG AGO, I was in a pub with my friends. After a few drinks, my friends told me that I wasn't a real writer because I only wrote textbooks on software testing.

"Really?" I exclaimed. "What do you want me to write?"

"A novel!" was their reply.

"About San Francisco!"

"And give the main characters our names!"

"OK," I said. "Give me a thousand dollars each and your names will live in eternity."

Naturally, the cheap suckers backed off. But I did write my first novel!

Alas, it's likely going to be my last one.

Would you like to know why? Because a real writer would never think to start his novel with a chapter titled *The History of Modern Capitalism.*

The History of Modern Capitalism

As was usual for me, all things came to either-or. Either I pass the finals and go on vacation, or I don't pass the finals and go into the Russian army.

Many people would kill to study where I did, at the Law School of Moscow State.

But I was dying of boredom. The entire freshman year was dedicated to theories, histories and abstractions that I just couldn't cram into my poor brain.

If you flunk out of college at the age of 19, you are drafted into the army. That was a solid reason to study hard. And I tried!

Somehow, I managed to take and pass all the finals, except the hardest exam, which I was facing next. It was strategically placed at the end, when we all were so exhausted that two years in the army began to sound like heaven.

That was an exam on the History of Modern Capitalism.

...

For two semesters, we had to forget about dorm

parties (and living in general), and dive into the centuries of class struggle in five countries: the United States, England, France, Japan, and Germany.

As expected, the most useless of courses was curated by the most fanatical professor. Her name was Victoria Shtein.

Professor Victoria loved her course like a mother loves a child—with passion, tenderness and jealousy. Those who didn't share her love were regarded as lazy asses and enemies of jurisprudence.

Among the lazy asses and enemies of jurisprudence that Professor Victoria had previously identified, I confidently held the top rank.

To be fair, I wasn't all that lazy, and I did like jurisprudence. I just couldn't make myself study something as utterly impractical as centuries of class struggle in five countries.

The only part of the course I knew—more or less—was The American Revolution, thanks to my term paper. It was about one percent of the course.

After concluding the last lecture, Professor Victoria responded to my "Goodbye" with "See you at the exam, soldier!"

"Not a soldier yet!" I replied and realized that my chances just dropped from one percent to zero.

The Professor's cursed exam was about to run me over like a train and only a miracle could save me.

Hence, I turned to student sorcery. The day before the exam, I went to the bronze statue of a dog at the subway station *Revolutionary Square* and rubbed its shiny nose to attract good luck.

Then, came the morning. And the good old method had worked again! Julie Kapustina, professor Victoria's young assistant, approached us at the doors of the exam room and announced the best news ever: professor Victoria was stuck in traffic! Hence, Julie would administer the exam herself.

I entered the classroom first as I always do. Fortune favors the brave, and a modest but dignified C- is a blessing if your fair grade is Z+.

An Exam

PROFESSOR VICTORIA knew by experience that the exam was a hopeless undertaking, so she dropped some Jesuitic slack into the process.

When a student entered the exam room, he saw a pile of tickets spread over the table. Each ticket lay face down and contained two questions. The student had to then flip a ticket and see if he could answer it. If he had no idea—which was usually the case—he could flip another one but his grade would drop one level down. That meant if he answered on B-, he got C- and so on.

I entered the exam room, said *hello* to Julie, and told her my full name—Roman Monin. Julie pointed me to the table and said, "Roman Monin, please, draw your ticket."

I flipped my first ticket: France and Japan. I looked at Julie. She nodded.

I flipped my second ticket: France and Germany. I looked at Julie. Again, she nodded.

Then came Germany and England. Julie nodded once again.

Then came France and the USA (a question regarding the abolition of slavery).

I couldn't remember saying anything more than "hello" to Julie for the entire year I had known her. But every time I saw her, my heart pounded as if it wanted to unhook itself from the arteries and my chest hurt as if an anaconda was trying to squash it. Alas, it didn't matter, because popular Julie showed no interest in me.

"Perhaps you would like to flip up all the tickets?" I heard her angel's voice.

Fortes fortuna adjuvat

"May I?" I responded.

Julie didn't reply. Instead, she walked to the

window and stared down at the well-packed traffic jam where professor Victoria was being cooked alive in her car, somewhere nearby.

It took me less than a minute to turn upside-down all tickets on the table to find one where both questions were about The American Revolution!

I answered without hesitation, got my undeserved C- and went to my friend Paust.

In Paust's Kitchen

I HAD MET VLAD PAUSTOVSKY just a year before at a prep class for the law school.

When he realized the future academic load, he said, "Fuck that shit!" and successfully applied to Moscow Polytechnic.

Paust was my best friend. Yet, he was jealous that I was studying at the top law school. That's why he called me a loser and used every opportunity to give me a guilt trip.

...

To celebrate my fiasco, Paust had ordered a keg of Guinness and was patiently waiting for my arrival—without pouring a single glass to himself.

"Finally! I almost died of dehydration!" he exclaimed as he greeted me at the doors.

At first, Paust was disappointed that I had passed the exam.

"You failed me, brother!" he said.

"Why?" I wondered.

"I've spent all day thinking about the arguments!"

"What arguments?"

"Why two years in trenches without booze and chicks are better than two years at the top law school."

But, after a glass of Guinness, Paust smiled and asked his wife, "Private, is the table ready?"

His wife, Marina, set up the table and we sat to celebrate.

...

The doorbell rang, just as we started our meal. Marina opened the door and invited the visitor into the kitchen. I turned my head to see... Julie! If Joan of Arc had ridden into the kitchen on her white horse, I'm sure I would have been less surprised.

Petrified, much like the Egyptian Sphinx, I let loose the spoon from my fingers and it dropped into hot borsch, shooting splatters of red, mostly towards Paust.

Paust squealed like a pig and jumped to the sink to quickly rinse his shirt.

By the time Julie arrived, I had already told the story of my brilliant performance during the exam but didn't know if Paust and Marina realized that it was Julie who had rescued me.

"Hello, I'm Julie!" she said as she smiled at me.

"Hello, I'm Roman," I mumbled and blushed.

I was so overwhelmed to see Julie in Paust's kitchen that I had no idea what to say or what to do. That's why I decided to play stupid and pretend that we had met only a minute prior.

"Julie girl," said Paust, "Check this out. This loser just passed his finals and, instead of the army, he is going...? By the way, Roman, where *are* you going?" he asked.

Then, he put on Hotel California at maximum volume and burst into dance, waving flaps of his shirt while trying to dry it.

The evening was easy, tranquil and warm. We just talked, laughed, ate and drank. Eventually, Marina and Paust retired to their bedroom, and Julie and I went to a vacant kids' room. Julie stretched on the couch, resting her head on my lap.

"Julie," I said, "you really saved me today. But why didn't you tell the guys that you knew me?"

"Roman," she replied, "it doesn't matter! Just kiss me."

So I did.

It's a Classic

SUDDENLY, there was a knock on the door, accompanied by the voice of an angry man.

"I know that she is here!" he exclaimed. "Her car is downstairs."

After the yelling and assorted commotion, the kid's room door was busted in and there was Paust, riding piggyback on some stranger.

"Roman!" he screeched. "Kill the fucker!"

I jumped from the couch, having no idea who the fucker was and why I had to kill him.

The stranger, a tall mate who appeared to be our age, lashed out like a wild mustang and threw Paust right into the toy box.

He then hissed at me, "Who the fuck are you, scum?" and, out of the blue, landed a jab to my eye.

"Who the fuck are *you*, scum?" I replied, as I submerged my fist into his fat belly.

The mystery man folded in half and Paust saddled up on him again, sparkling like lightning in his bright orange boxers.

They both dropped to the floor.

"Fuck you, bitches!" the stranger cried. "Let me go, fucker!"

Paust weakened his grip. His opponent jumped up, spit on Paust and ran away.

I dressed and also headed to the door.

Julie tried to stop me.

"Roman, please, don't leave!" she pleaded.

"Sorry, Julie," I responded. "But I'm not a toy to be played with!"

"Can't you stay just for a minute?" she asked in despair.

"I'm leaving."

I didn't recognize myself. But my anger was so

strong and disappointment so painful that I didn't want to get anything sorted out.

"Then take this with you," she said as she kissed me on the neck.

I stopped for just a second, realizing that I shouldn't leave, and I left.

Sparrow

I MANAGED to make it home early in the morning.

At the entrance to my apartment building, I stumbled on a familiar character, with a huge black Labrador.

"Sparrow!" I called out.

"Roman!"

It was my old friend Alex "The Sparrow." Nobody could quite remember how Alex had become The Sparrow, but nobody called him anything else, including his single dad.

"What's up with your mug?" he asked.

"Business as usual, a gentle night," I replied. "What's up with you?"

"Walking with Lady! Adorable beast, isn't she?"

"Oh, yes!" I replied, looking at her impressive size. "Man, I'm so thirsty."

"Well, if it works," he suggested, "I have some fruit wine. What do you say?"

"Let's go!"

...

And there were truth and remedy in that wine.

After several glasses, we giggled, remembering our school years. At some point, I told Sparrow about my exam, Julie and the mystery man I assumed to be her boyfriend.

"Roman," Sparrow said, "I just don't know. You should've at least listened to her. Even if she slept with you just for fun, she is not your property, right?"

"Of course, not," I replied. "I wasn't myself, bro. Maybe the History of Modern Capitalism did that to me?"

"Then call her!" he demanded.

"And what I'm gonna say?"

"Just talk to her," he insisted. "It's quite normal, you know."

"Sparrow, listen," I said. "Your dad still makes a moonshine, right?"

"Right! Want some?"

"Let's go!"

It's Never a Bad Time for Glorious Ideas

AFTER not a small amount of moonshine, Sparrow was ready for action.

"Roman, listen," he said, "let's go to Paust!"

"What for?" I asked.

"First of all, we'll bring some moonshine. Maybe Julie will come!"

He did have a point. So, I called Paust.

"Roman!" Paust screeched. "Where the fuck are ya? Hurry up, brother, and get here now!"

"What's up?" I replied.

"Marina and Julie are staging a coup!" he complained. "They are hugging, crying and howling that all men—especially you and me—are pigs. Looks like the words will be ending soon and then the chicks will start scratching out my eyes."

"We are coming!" I said.

"We who?" Paust asked.

"Sparrow, Lady and I."

"Perfect! Wait! Is lady a chick?"

"No, a labrador!"

"Exactly what I need!" he replied.

Paust then yelled to girls, "Behold, feminists! The Lady is coming!"

What followed was the sound of smack and Paust screaming, "Why?" Then, he hung up.

Sparrow and I made it to the subway and somehow managed to pass the calf-sized Lady through the security gate.

"Sparrow," I said, "let's drink for every station of our wonderful Moscow subway!"

"Let's go!"

Hello, Dolly!

WHEN I finally regained my consciousness, I was sitting on a chair, handcuffed. Somebody was hitting my back with a rubber baton. With a great effort, I turned my head and saw... Julie's boyfriend in a police uniform. He noticed a glimpse of sanity in my eyes, sat in front of me and declared with pure joy, "Welcome to the kingdom of pain, you moron! Lieutenant Arthur Parigin is at your service!"

I tried to get my thoughts in order. It wasn't easy. There was a blank spot in my memory about everything that had happened between the first subway station and now.

I blinked several times, trying to focus my eyes.

Behind Lieutenant Parigin was a cage with Sparrow in it. It looked like we had moonshined ourselves straight into the subway jail.

"Hey, you!" Parigin yelled at me.

"Dude," I said, "I had no idea that Julie is your girlfriend. Is she your girlfriend?"

"I don't give a fuck what you think!" he bellowed. "I've known Julie for years! Our parents went to college together.

We have it all planned, do you understand? Planned!"

Gulping for breath, he continued.

"You are finished! I'm gonna put you and this dumbass into the system," he said as he pointed to sobbing Sparrow. "And you'll take a long trip for resisting arrest."

"For resisting arrest?" I asked.

"Look at Boris!"

His colleague, Boris, a typical bleary-eyed subway cop, sat in the corner. His face was bruised, and his shirt torn up as if he just came from the bar brawl. He drank Sparrow's moonshine right from the bottle and, raising it bottom-up, looked like a trumpet player in exile.

"He just tried talking to you drunk pigs," Parigin continued, "and your friend set his mutt on him."

"You mean, a big black lab?" I asked.

"Yes, a big black lab. That creature bit Boris and then you both beat him up."

Boris released a sniff as if confirming his colleague's words. A crying and shaken Sparrow jumped from the bench in the cell and yelled, "Lady didn't bite anybody!"

Lady was nowhere in the room.

"Listen," I asked Parigin, "What can we do? Yes, we fucked up, but do you really want to put us in jail? Sparrow never hurt anyone in his life."

"I don't give a fuck!" came his angry reply. "You go down and he joins you, or he goes down and you join him. Take it as you want, I don't care. I'll be back in five and we'll put you into the system."

The first rule when you get arrested is to resolve things as quickly as possible. After papers are filed and gears of the man-eating machine start to roll, the price of freedom will increase every day and, at some point, nothing can be done anymore.

I realized that Boris was our only chance.

"Boris," I said, "please, forgive us! I don't remember what happened, but we are idiots. Please, let me make a call."

"Hahaha! You watched too many American movies."

"Can something be done?" I asked.

"Yes," he replied. "You can start learning jailbird jargon, hehe!"

"I have forty bucks on me," I informed him. "It's all yours if you will just let me make a call."

Sparrow's moonshine was a potent thing, and the opportunity to grab a little extra cash warmed up the cop's heart like a Caribbean wave.

"All righty," he said, "what's the number?"

I gave him Paust's number. After dialing, Boris put his cell phone to my ear.

"Paust," I said, "we are in the subway jail. Here reins the moron that you rode yesterday. We are in big trouble!"

"OK, I'm calling my dad."

...

Paust's dad, Leon Paustovsky, was something of a big shot in the General Prosecutor's Office. He belonged to the old cohort of commie leaders who—not only survived the transition to capitalism in the devastating nineties—but also got more prosperous and more powerful along the way. This is a closed club and there are no strangers there. The law is made for simpletons while Leon and his circle can sort out any problem just making a phone call.

...

Parigin returned to the room.

"Hey, what's up!!" he exclaimed as he snatched the phone from Boris's hand.

"Do you know Leon, Paust's father?" I asked.

"So what?" he replied. "It doesn't change anything! It's me who is the king here!"

"Where is Lady, you piece of shit?" Sparrow yelled at him.

"What?" Parigin yelled back, taking his baton from the table, "You think it's all a joke? I've made sure that they'll put that beast of yours down today."

Sparrow hung on the metal bars of the cell and started to weep. He wept like a child, trembling and sobbing. Tears didn't flow down from his eyes, they sprinkled forward.

Parigin's cell phone rang.

"Yes, Leon. They resisted arrest. No, nothing like that. OK, then."

He hung up, aimed the baton at my shoulder and gave me a savory hit for the road.

"Hey you," he continued, "Boris the traitor. Let them go."

Boris, apparently now a traitor, volunteered to see us off. When we got outside, he stretched his arm and demanded, "Give me my money!"

"Where is Lady?" I asked him.

"What lady?"

"My friend's black lab."

"At the pound."

"Where 'at the pound'?"

"Down the street," he pointed his finger.

"If I give you the money, how would I bail out Lady?" I asked. "Or is Lady's life not worth forty bucks?"

Sparrow interrupted me, "Roman, just pay him. I got some money on me from the moonshine sales."

I drew two twenties from my pocket but held on to them.

"Boris, what really happened?" I asked.

"I wanted to arrest you," he said. "But you hit me and he told the dog to 'take him.' That's when it bit me."

Sparrow waved his hands in protest, "Lady never bites," he said. "She doesn't even know the command 'take him.' Roman, just give him the money! Let this be over."

After we compensated Boris the traitor for his kindnesses, he went back to catch more criminals, and I parted with Sparrow.

"Roman," Sparrow said, "I'm going to bail Lady out, and you should get yourself over to Paust's. Let's sync up in the evening."

"Bye, bro."

Poor Hedgehog Shrinking

J ULIE had left by the time I made it to the Pausts. Marina took off my shirt to inspect my injuries and revealed a lilac bruise, half the size of my back. Marina sighed, poured cold water into a bowl and started to wipe my heroic wounds with a moist cloth.

Paust had already recovered his alcohol level with leftovers from the Guinness keg. He was calmly rocking in the chair, drilling the ceiling with his foggy eyes.

"No worries!" he assured me. "Daddy will get things sorted. Want a cerveza?"

"No, gracias. I've had enough," was my reply. "So, how do you know that cop, Parigin?"

"Our families used to be close," he explained. "Then, he got crazy because of his obsession with Julie. He dropped out of college, beat up one of Julie's colleagues in the middle of the lecture, totaled his father's car, and so on and so forth. His folks were ashamed of him. They distanced themselves from us."

"So, he is not Julie's boyfriend?" I asked.

"I don't think so. She used to ignore him, but they are cool now. By the way, yesterday, she came especially to see you, dumb ass."

"Especially to see me?!"

"Yep! I told her about you and she got interested."

"Did you give her my last name?" I asked. "Did you tell her that I'm in the same law school?"

"Of course!" he chirped back. "You are not wanted by the state—yet! Haha! So, it was *she* who saved your ass?"

"Who else?" I wondered back. "I was hoping that you'd turn your brain on. She was making fun of you, but you kept rinsing your shirt like some possessed raccoon."

Paust threw an evil look to Marina, "You too, Brutus? Are you with them or with me?"

"My dear," answered Marina, "I'm always with you. But how could I miss another awkward act of your *I Care Only About Myself* play?"

"Fine, you sneaky conspirators!" came Paust's retort. "One day honest people will prevail!"

Paust looked at me with pity and continued in a preaching tone of voice, "By the way, you've really offended Julie. There is nothing dumber than leaving a girl like her the way you did it."

I was swept over with happiness! Let Paust curse and swear—I didn't care. But yesterday Julie came to see *me* and she risked her entire career to save me!

At that moment, Paust's niece, Arisha, entered the living room.

"May I read a poem to uncle Roman?" she asked.

"No!" Paust retorted. "Go back to your room. Can't you see? Uncle Roman fell down the stairs."

Marina looked at him with undisguised contempt and said, "It's you who will fall down the stairs if you continue to drink so much."

She then encouraged Arisha, "We are listening, my princess!"

Arisha climbed on a stool and recited,

"Poor hedgehog is shrinking,
Nothing he can do,
His crooked face is tingling,
And his skin turned blue.
His mama can't stop sobbing,
She cannot stop to cry,
Her son's no longer calling,
And worries multiply."

With a curtsy, Arisha looked at us, expecting well-deserved applause.

Marina's hand got away from my blue back. Over the bowl of cold water came the drip-drop, drip-drop into the silence.

I looked at Paust, then at Marina.

Crazy energy exploded between us and we started to laugh like never before.

Paust and I fell to the floor, squirming in fits and howling like madmen. Paust was snorting, wheezing and crying at the same time. He pointed his finger at me, trying to say, "A hedgehog," but could only produce something akin to "meh-meh-meh."

Unable to speak, he ended up rolling on the carpet, spraying saliva and rubbing his wet eyes with his fists.

Marina, nearly suffocating on the chair and covering her face with her palms, waved to an amazed Arisha that she could go.

Even after several minutes, when the worst was over, we tried not to glance at each other in hopes of preventing the next round. It was a sea, NO, an ocean of happiness! There was no more Parigin, no more pain, no more fear. Joy and carelessness of youth came gushing from our hearts like a sparkling fountain, and we swam in love with each other.

It was then that I realized who else I needed there. Who I needed then and for the rest of my life.

I knew that I would do anything just to be with her.

"Paust," I begged, "please call Julie. I'm such an idiot and I'm so happy!"

"Aye aye, sir!" he replied.

But before Paust could make his way to the phone, it rang on its own. Paust picked up and answered, "Yes, he is here."

"Roman," Paust said, "go downstairs. My dad's car is waiting for you."

I ran to the elevator. It was there that I encountered a very large man, sporting a special police uniform and blocking my way.

At the Leon's Den

A<small>RE YOU</small> R<small>OMAN</small> M<small>ONIN</small>?" he asked.

"Yes."

"I'm taking you to Leon Paustovsky," he told me. "Give me your hand."

Then, he handcuffed our wrists together.

"Why are you doing this?" I asked him in surprise.

The scornful glance he gave me was as if I'd asked him to wash my socks. From that point, I had no more questions.

We got into the back seat of black BMW and took off. After a short time, the car pulled over near a two-story building that had no identifying plaque at the entrance. The big guy took me to the basement, and we entered a small, clean cell with a table and two chairs. A single, naked light bulb on the ceiling emitted a yellow soft light. He uncuffed me.

"Wait here," he barked.

The door closed behind him and the lock clicked home.

I had no clue what was going on. But I had no

doubts that, after an unpleasant talk with Leon, I would be released, everything would be forgotten, like a nightmare, and I would return Julie's kiss later that day.

The lock clicked, the door opened, and Leon Paustovsky entered the cell.

"Hello, Leon!" I cheerfully greeted him.

"Hello, hello," he answered in a cold, unimpressed tone.

"Leon, why?" I pointed to the cell walls.

"Roman," he said, "do I look like a janitor to you?"

"No."

"And yet," he continued, "I've been cleaning up your shit since this morning. Arthur Parigin and

Boris Klimenko assert that your pal set his dog on Boris. Then, both of you beat him up and ran away from the subway police station."

"I talked to Arthur's father and Arthur himself," he went on. "His father cannot make Arthur change his mind. Arthur is in love with Julie and I cannot do much to help you—except for one thing."

I listened closely.

"I will give you 24 hours to leave the country," he said. "If you comply, both you and your pal will be fine. If you leave, there is no case and no harm. If you stay or return, they'll jail you and your friend for many many years. And I'll help them."

"You will help them?" I asked, unable to believe my ears.

"Yes, and there is one more condition."

"One more?"

"Forget Julie," he said. "Your life is ruined already, and I will not allow you to ruin her life as well. I don't really care about you, Roman. I'm helping you because my son asked me to. But I do care about Julie. I have known her from the day she was born and I wish her only happiness."

I was barely able to process what I was being told.

"You cannot give her happiness," he continued. "You can only hurt her.

"Like elders say: out of sight, out of the heart. In a year, you both will forget each other, and your paths will never cross again."

"But may I call her?" I asked.

"Not even once!" he bellowed. "Just one contact with her and your friend, Sparrow, goes to jail. That's our agreement and my promise to you. No contacts with Julie! Don't even try to ask my son to call her. By the way, show me your fists."

I did and he examined them.

"Strange," he puzzled. "You have neither bruises nor sores. When was the last time you hit somebody?"

"I recently hit Parigin," I replied, "but his stomach was too soft to bruise a fist."

"Well, funny guy," he hissed at me, "it doesn't matter now."

"What matters is that your word means nothing against the word of police officers—one of whom has a very powerful father. Even if you'll eventually get acquitted, you'll leave the jail in a wheelchair. We don't make it easy for people who assault us."

"Here is what you're gonna do," he continued. "Go home, get money and a passport, and then take a taxi to the airport for international flight wherever. And don't be stupid. No tricks. No plays."

"What about my parents?" I asked.

"Call them after you land. All clear?"

"Yes," I said, "all clear."

"Then go."

...

It was surreal.

My whole life had exploded and shattered into sharp, bleeding particles.

I had screwed up everyone I loved and everything I had.

But even in the darkest hour, I couldn't help myself and smiled when I realized that never again would I have to take another exam on the freaking History of Modern Capitalism.

Mary, It's a Go

M Y PARENTS were at work. I packed my passport, money, for some reason a tennis racket, and a change of underwear into my backpack. From the street, I called my former classmate, who worked at a tour agency.

"Mary," I said, "it's Roman Monin. I need a ticket for an international flight to wherever and I need it now."

"Hahaha!" Mary chortled. "I recognize your style, Monin! Give me a minute."

Well, stupid me! Just yesterday, I was a student at a top law school. Just yesterday, I made love with the most beautiful girl in the world. But, overnight, I turned into an outlaw and now I cannot even call Julie.

"Hey, Monin!" Mary said, returning to the line. "I have a ticket to San Francisco for eight pm. Two thousand dollars."

"But I don't have a visa to the United States!"

"What do you mean?" she asked. "I got it for you last year. Don't you remember that you wanted to see New York?"

I sighed with relief. Now, the problem was money.

My entire fortune was 2,200 dollars. That meant I would arrive—with a mere 200 dollars and my very basic English—to a city where nobody was waiting for me and where I knew no one.

"Mary," I said, "it's a go."

With a pounding heart and fully expecting to be cuffed and thrown in jail, I passed through customs at the airport and fell into a chair at my gate.

The fear had evaporated and the emptiness inside of me filled with shame. I had betrayed everyone I knew and I would never deserve their forgiveness.

The boarding started. I made my way to my seat on the plane and passed out.

Welcome to the United States of America

B OY, you sure can snore!"

Next to me sat a smiling, chubby, Russian guy in his thirties.

He continued, "Where are you going?"

"San Francisco," I responded.

"Wow! You wanna see the Bridge?"

"Maybe," I replied. "I'm gonna see my friends."

"Really? What are their names? Where do they live? I know everyone in the City."

"They just arrived," I said. "I don't know where they live."

"How long are you going to stay?"

"I really don't know," I replied with some irritation. "Sorry, man. I don't feel well."

"That's cool. I'm Shmagy, by the way."

"I'm Roman."

...

After some time dozing, I was awakened by Shmagy's voice, "Wake up, bro!"

Our Boeing appeared to be descending straight into the San Francisco Bay. But, at the last moment, the landing strip appeared out of nowhere and we sat on the promised land of the United States of America.

...

After deplaning, I got in line for non-residents. The immigration officer looked with suspicion at my modest belongings.

"What is the purpose of your visit?" he asked.

"I'm a student. I'm studying The Revolution."

"Mexican?"

"Why Mexican?" I was puzzled. "Of the United States."

"And what does California have to do with that?"

At that moment, I realized that I would have to come up with a lie. And not just any lie. But a solid and believable lie that would convince him and even myself.

"Fort Ross has records," I managed. "You know. The Boston tea party. Russian sailors."

He looked at me with compassion. Then he sighed and stamped my passport.

"Welcome to the United States of America."

Shmagy

WHEN I STEPPED OUTSIDE, a gust of fresh wind hit my face. I stopped and took it in, feeling as though I couldn't breathe enough of it. It wasn't just a wind. It was a wind of hope, a wind of new, a wind of... possible happiness!

Hello, America! Here I am!

A black Lexus pulled over next to me.

"So," said Shmagy, "nobody is meeting you?"

"No."

Shmagy got out of the car, collected my belongings and threw them into the back seat.

"Spend a night at my place," he proposed. "And tomorrow we'll figure something out."

Shmagy lived at Fulton and 20th Avenue in a house that was used as a dorm. One room had neither furniture nor a tenant. Shmagy gave me a yoga mat.

"Still better than the cold floor," he said.

"How much do I owe you for the night?" I asked.

"Are you crazy?" he snorted. "It's a gift from my big heart!"

I looked around, dropped my backpack on the floor and asked, "Shmagy, may I check my email on your computer?"

"Sure!" he replied. "The username is *shmagy* and the password is *sex*."

I had three messages in my inbox: one from Paust, one from my mom and one from Julie.

Paust informed me that Parigin had sworn to find me and break my neck.

My mother asked me to call her, indicating to me that Paust had told her everything.

Julie explained that she knew everything and that she wouldn't count on a reply from me. I typed a reply, then deleted it, then started all over. But a thought was stuck in my brain like a splinter. It was something Paust's father had said.

Foggy Park

I WENT OUTSIDE, crossed Fulton and found myself in the park.

Majestic eucalyptuses were drawing themselves out of the fog as I went on. The chilly air was filled with a strong pharmaceutical aroma. A lone seagull splashed the lake, took off with a clang, and disappeared in the shadows. And once again, a silence fell around me.

It was so beautiful, so tranquil and like a fairytale.

Where are you, Julie? If only you knew how much I want to hug you, return your kiss and share this fairytale with you!

And then I realized what had been tormenting me. Julie's life was already set: elite school, a marriage with a man from a prominent family, prestigious work—if she ever wanted to work. But most importantly, she had almost guaranteed security and well-being. And I had almost ruined it for her.

What kind of security or well-being could I possibly provide? What kind of future awaited her with the likes of me? Leon was right about everything.

I had already wrecked my own life, and the last

thing I wanted to do was to drag Julie along with me into the abyss.

Something squeezed my chest so hard that I could barely breathe.

An old man, clothed in a down parka and a knitted peaky cap, came out of the fog. I asked him, "Hello, where is the ocean?"

He looked at me with disdain and answered with a thick Russian accent, "Fuck that ocean. And fuck you too."

Then, he creaked by and disappeared into the fog, just like the seagull.

Miss Lee and Mister Antonio

THE FOLLOWING MORNING, we had a visitor: Miss Lee, Shmagy's no-nonsense landlady. Miss Lee issued a stare at the yoga mat and my backpack before curtly announcing,

"Five hundred dollars a month. And another five hundred for the deposit."

"He only has two hundred," Shmagy answered on my behalf.

"What?" she asked in surprise.

"But he can work for you to pay the balance."

"Okay," she replied. "Let him change and get to work."

I had nothing to change into. Shmagy gave me his old jogging pants, a t-shirt with a cute pink pony on it and a pair of holey sneakers.

I went outside and saw a luxury Mercedes belonging to Miss Lee and a barely-holding-up pickup truck with an old Chinese man behind the wheel.

I was instructed by Miss Lee's finger to go to the pickup truck, and we took off to work on her house in Sunset.

The construction crew was made up of Chinese and Mexicans. We worked on the walls, first applying a primer, then leveling it with sandpaper. The Chinese men were rather reserved, but the Mexicans accepted me like their own and were soon teaching me how to swear in Spanish.

When lunchtime arrived, the Mexicans and I ate at the Vietnamese cafe at Irving and 19th Avenue. I don't remember the name of the place, but I remember that it had a *2* in it.

It was there that I first experienced what was surely the tastiest thing in the world: Vietnamese Pho Bo.

To pay for my meal, I tried to sell my wristwatch to my colleagues. Instead of accepting my proposal, they recommended that I stick it up my ass and chipped in a dollar each to pay for my soup.

At 4:00 pm that afternoon, Miss Lee showed me two twenties. Before I could even reach for them, she quickly put them back into her purse.

"You owe me 960 bucks, OK?" she said.

"OK," I replied.

"Be here tomorrow at eight. OK?"

"OK."

...

All covered in white dust, like a Christmas tree with snow, I walked home, using the crimson tips of the Golden Gate Bridge as guidance. I looked so out of place that passersby kept stopping to stare at me, trying to decide what would suit me better—a shower, a policeman or an urgent psychiatric intervention.

Not expecting such a shock, poor Shmagy sprang backward when he opened the door.

I spent half of the evening in the shower getting rid of the small, sharp particles of primer stuck into my skin, hair, ears and nose. The clothes that Shmagy had given me in the morning were mostly ruined, but I couldn't afford the luxury of throwing them away. So, I spent the second half of the evening trying to wash them.

"Shmagy," I asked, "can you lend me 200 bucks?"

"Of course I can," he answered. "How was it today?"

"¡Muy perfecto!" I replied. "It wasn't for nothing that I studied History of Modern Capitalism."

"Oh, boy!" he chirped. "You seem like a sharp guy, and Miss Lee is happy with you, but come on! Do something smart."

"Maybe *you* could tell me what that smart something is?" I asked.

"Sure! Coding!" he replied with enthusiasm. "Coding is smart! During the gold rush, people came to California to find gold. But now it's time to make money on salaries and stock options. Look how much I make!"

He showed me a check, made out to him for 4000 dollars.

"And I get that every two weeks!" he explained with pride. "Plus, there are tons of stock options."

"What is a stock option?"

"It's the right to buy the stocks of your company at a low, fixed price. But you have to work for that company for at least one year. The difference between the stock option price and the market stock price is your gain."

"But what if the stock option price is higher than the market stock price?" I asked.

Shmagy winced as if I had poked him with a cattle prod, and he whispered, "Let's not talk about it. Let's not push such horrible ideas into the cosmos."

Later that evening, Shmagy introduced me to Antonio Gorsky, the owner of a restaurant called

Russian Idea. Antonio grinned when Shmagy told him how we had met.

"My dear friend," he said, "how do you like San Francisco so far? I bet you thought that Sharon Stone would grab you from the plane and start seducing you with sex, drugs and rock-n-roll, hehe. And you are like, 'No, Sharon! Thank you. I'm tired.'

"But in reality, nobody met you at the airport, you sleep on the floor, and you will wait tables at Russian Idea. Sure, it made sense to come here. But, in general, welcome to America!"

That's how I got two jobs in one day.

Wake Up, Work Out, Fall Down

F OR THE FIRST WEEKS, I functioned like a robot. I woke up in the morning, went to work, worked for twelve hours, came back home, and turned myself off for the night. No reflections. No hopes. No plans.

On the plus side, hard physical labor not only distracted my mind but also gave me a new perspective.

I met men who had been illegal migrants for years, and, whoever didn't want to pay an official minimum, could hire them to do the hardest work. What seemed as semi-slavery to me was a blessing to them, because—in their native countries—the situation was even worse.

The six bucks bowl of Pho was a luxury and a celebration they could afford only once a month. These men tried to save on everything, sending as much money as they could to their families back home. They were poor, uneducated peasants, rough tongued and heartful at the same time. And all of them shared two dreams: bringing their families to the States and giving their children a good education.

I didn't have any dreams. I just wanted to survive and pay off my debt to Shmagy. Soon, the debt grew even bigger because Smagy bought me an old Dell laptop. I said that I couldn't accept it only to hear, "Throw it in the garbage, if you can't."

An Ocean Race, Damn It

Every evening, we met in the kitchen, both exhausted. I suffered from twelve hours of physical work while Shmagy suffered from disagreement with his company's hiring policy.

"Check this out, man!" he exclaimed. "What absolute dumb asses! They keep hiring clueless Java noobs who make Baby Jesus cry. Instead of raising my salary! 'We need more programmers'—they say. Fuck that! How are you?"

"This sucks," I replied. "My amigo, Luis, caught a brick in the head. Blood was all over the place. But he doesn't have health insurance and went home with patches on his head."

Shmagy looked at me with fleeting concern and then continued.

"By the way," he said, "call Antonio and tell him that you are taking Sunday off. We are going to the ocean race to Farallon Islands."

"But I know nothing about sailing!" I objected.

"You don't need to," assured Shmagy. "Just do what they say and watch for the boom, because it can crush your skull like a nut."

"Is it gonna rock?"

"Just a little."

...

Puke started to come out of my face like water out of a firehose the moment we reached the ocean. Back in the Bay, the waters were calm and I was doing all right. But after we passed under the Bridge, the waves got bigger and bigger. Soon, they turned into moving hills. Our sailboat was going up and down those hills.

Each up motion twisted my guts into a rope, and each down motion ejected whatever was at the top of the queue. First out was my breakfast, followed by the KFC chicken I'd had for dinner, then came morsels of my stomach and, maybe, of lungs.

The sailboat was heeling, and I sprawled myself on the lower side like a wet mop, submerging my twisted face into the sparkling splashes. That was how I spent four unforgettable hours.

When we reached the Farallon Islands, I was somewhere between the realms of the living and the dead, probably closer to the dead side. All I could do was keep my eyes half-open while watching the monstrous waves crash against the coastal cliffs.

Shmagy paid me a visit and handed me a can of ginger ale.

"By the way," he said, "these waters have more great whites than Silicon Valley has Java noobs!"

"Great whites?"

"Great white sharks," he responded. "They love to munch on humans!"

"Bue-e-e-e-e..."

...

We rounded the islands on port, and nothing portended yet another misfortune. But what seemed like the end turned out to be the beginning. One of the guys on board, Hugh, suggested installing a spinnaker. This is a sail that looks like a bubble at the front of the sailboat.

Men decided and men did. But, alas, they did it like idiots. We retrieved the spinnaker from the hold and tried to install it.

"We're gonna fly like eagles! Like eagles! Like eagles!" Hugh sang, looking with happy wonder at the spinnaker tackle. Just like me, he had no idea.

Out of the blue, the sky turned black and a roaring squall hit our boat. Strong gusts tore the partly-tied spinnaker from our hands and it unfolded somewhere on the side. Pulled by the spinnaker, our boat jerked left and rolled at almost 90 degrees. Everything that was on the deck slid down into the ocean, including our crew.

I grabbed a lifeline with a death grip and hung above the foamy water. Shmagy, Hugh and Captain Rob were hanging alongside. My nausea vanished without a trace, and I was promising God that I would be a good boy from now until forever. Shmagy, pale like death, was promising the same.

Captain Rob managed to reach into his pocket for a serrated knife and cut off the spinnaker line.

Our boat leveled.

Barely standing on his stiff legs, Shmagy poked his bluish finger into Hugh's face and said what we all wanted to say, "Fuck you, fucking fucked up fuck."

We set up our regular sails, and I assumed my regular position, rolling over the afterdeck and rattling like a wounded antelope.

Fortunately, the wind was fair, and soon, the shimmering lights on the East welcomed us back to the City of disco.

A Hope

Driving home, Shmagy and I forgot our well-meant promises and engaged in a heated discussion over what bar we needed to visit.

My body felt like a punching bag, but my spirits were high. The drive that I got from a near-death experience and rescue ignited something in me. Our miraculous survival gave me hope about another miracle: seeing Julie once again. I thought about her every day.

"Shmagy," I said, "I don't wanna paint walls for the rest of my life. What should I do?"

"Learn to code!" he replied.

"How?"

"Do coding!"

Shmagy went to his bedroom and brought me two books: *Python for Idiots* and *C++ for Dummies* and told me, "Find some tasks and projects for yourself and do coding. That's the only way."

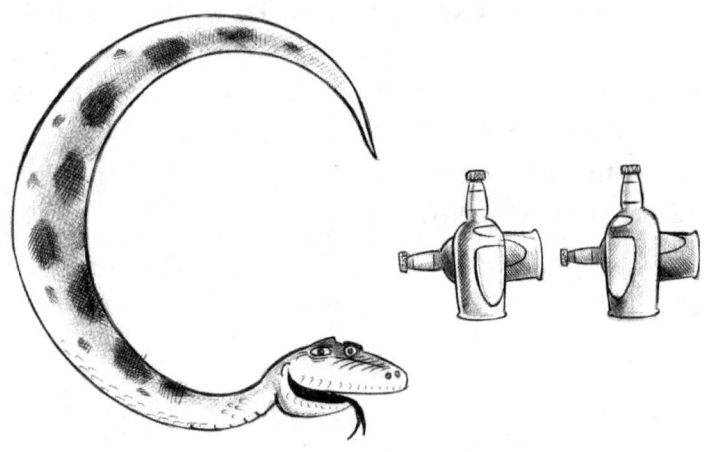

Do Coding

M Y HIGH SCHOOL COMPUTER TEACHER was a woman named Isolde, but we called her Tristan. She hated computers, considering them mere physical objects with buttons, wires and monitors. She did, however, love algorithms, logic and—(God forbid!)—discrete math, and that was exactly what she taught us.

Every computer lesson started with turning off our computers and turning on our brains. Everyone had to work hard, participate and solve things. By the end of the 45-minute lesson, our brains were hurting like sore muscles.

Back then, we loathed Tristan for her tyranny. But I now realized that my pain hadn't been for nothing. Both Python and C++ felt natural to me and pierced easily into my brain, swollen by theories and abstractions. Unlike theory, however, practical coding was enjoyable and even magical, because I could create something new and see the results right away.

Soon, Shmagy helped me to install Ubuntu on my laptop, and I began learning Vim and the command line.

If anyone could abuse a good thing, it was me. Whatever I was doing, I'd always think about algorithms, regular expressions, databases and coding challenges. I became a fanatic, a nerd, losing interest in everything not related to programming.

Shmagy was both impressed with my progress and worried about me at the same time. I was beginning to look like a zombie because of sleep deprivation and all the load from construction, table waiting and computer studies. Even Antonio became concerned and would pack me a bag of kebabs, potatoes and salad after my shifts at his restaurant.

One day, after I had passed out and fallen from

my chair, Shmagy confiscated my laptop and exclaimed, "That's it!"

We then went to the pub in North Beach where
we got so wasted that we couldn't explain to the
taxi driver where we lived.

Yes, I Can!

O F COURSE, I didn't stop programming. Instead of coding on the computer, I was coding in my notepad. But I did begin what Shmagy would consider a proper lifestyle. Every evening, we drank beer, ate junk food and watched a movie. Soon, I was forgiven my transgressions and received my laptop back.

One day, Shmagy decided to test my programming skills by asking me to write two programs with the same functionalities using Python and C++.

When I called him after an hour, he tried to calm me down, "It's OK. I would give up too."

"I didn't give up," I answered and launched both of my programs for him to see. They worked precisely as they should.

"This is impossible," he exclaimed. "I would not have been able to do it better."

It seemed my friend was equal parts upset and proud at the same time.

"We should find you a proper job," he pronounced.

"But I don't have employment authorization," I said.

"Ha!" he winked. "Who has?"

"You."

"Of course, I have! I have lived here ten freaking years!"

"So, what can I do?" I asked.

"There are only two ways for bums like us: ask for asylum or marry an American chick. Have you been oppressed in Russia?"

"In a way," I said.

"Do you have any scars or something?" Shmagy asked.

"My heart is scarred."

"Well, hehe, that doesn't count. All right, you need to marry," he said with confidence.

"But I have somebody in Russia," I replied.

"It doesn't matter. It's a pure formality!" Shmagy looked at me like he was telling an obvious thing.

"No, bro, I have somebody already and I'll marry only her," I said firmly.

"Well, I don't like arguing with fools," he winced. "If you don't want my help, best of luck."

"I want your help. I just need something else."

Shmagy had an Aha! moment then.

"Wait, there is a third way! You have to register a corporation and do corp-to-corp work. In other words, you work for your corporation, and your corporation signs a contract with a software company."

"Is it even legal?" I asked.

"Everything is legal until they catch your illegal ass, muahaha!" Shmagy was having a good time once again.

"That's inspiring," I sneered.

"Bro, if you don't marry for documents, corp-to-corp is your only way," he assured me.

"And how do I register my corporation?"

"Google and you shall retrieve. By the way, tell me about your girl."

I told him about everything that had happened in Moscow.

"Yeah," he said. "I suspected something like that but didn't want to bug you. Do you really love her so much?"

"Yes, and I don't want to give her to that fucking Parigin," I replied.

"Ok, ok, you register your corp and I'll arrange your interview."

The Interview

SHMAGY didn't waste any time. Within two days, I received a request for a phone screening.

Silicon Valley had more money than people who could type "Hello World!"—to say nothing of decent coders. Recruiters stalked, hunted and courted them, raising the stakes up and up until it would be insane to refuse the job offer.

I didn't have the experience to be a decent coder. But when Shmagy told his boss, Prashant, that a decent Python programmer was looking for a job, the process started immediately.

The phone screening took about 20 minutes, and I was soon invited to a face-to-face interview.

At the beginning of the interview, I was flushed, sweaty and shaking, but my worries proved groundless. The interviewers asked me about standard algorithms and gave me coding challenges on sorting that I could solve without much effort.

The problem was not in programming, but in communication. All my interviewers were from India, and at first, we couldn't understand each other. Soon though, the curves of Russian and Indian accents synced up without our even noticing the phonetic monster that we had summoned.

Two days later, Prashant called me and offered a contract. I emailed him my company's details and started work the following Monday.

I was actually working at a software company in Silicon Valley! The guy who slept on the floor at the dorm and, only yesterday, had been hauling heavy bricks for Miss Lee and running with hot plates at *Russian Idea*!

```python
if stay_in_Russia == True:
  life = "prison for Roman"

elif call_Julie == True:
  life = "prison for Sparrow"

else:
  life = "San Francisco"
```

Restless Jessica

MY NEW COMPANY was called NN, Inc., and it was located near the swamps on Embarcadero Road in Palo Alto. Almost all of their coders were recent immigrants from India, China and Russia. Americans did product management, business development and accounting.

Then there was HR Jessica, who sincerely hated us newcomers. Her ancestors had arrived to the promised land on the Mayflower, and it was on that basis that she regarded herself as a special human edition. Better than us, of course.

The true American knew the ropes and tried not to express her views out loud. But judging by her face, we were stabbing her in the heart every time we thanked her for our fat paychecks in our colorful, foreign accents, "Sank u, Gesika!"

Barely thirty seconds had ticked by since I'd stepped into the NN Inc. office when she requested my social security number and my green card. I made an offended face and told her that I didn't have a green card because I was an American citizen. She responded that my United States passport would suffice as an alternative, and I promised to bring it the next day.

I kept feeding her with 'mañanas' for a week. After a few days, she knew that something was wrong, and a heart-warming opportunity to fuck me up made her wait for me at the reception every morning, where she would greet me with a taunting, "Where is your passport, Roman?"

Our African-American receptionist, Portia, trying to defend me, would tell Jessica to leave me alone, only to hear, "Mind your own business!"

I shared the problem with Shmagy.

Shmagy invited Jessica over for a sushi dinner.

The sushi dinner concluded at our apartment, with the entire building shaking the whole night like a torture chamber because of the violent pounding and loud moans.

Shmagy was a good programmer, to be certain. But his true talent lay in a different realm. He had an inexplicable, potent charisma that many women just couldn't resist. He was a stocky guy with a plain face, but his soft voice and piercing eyes did magic that no one can simply learn—either you have the gift or you don't.

In the morning, while I was munching on sushi leftovers, a shining Jessica floated into the kitchen. She kissed me on the cheek and told me that she wanted to convert to *Russianity*.

"I'm 26 years old," she said, "but I haven't lived! Tell me, Roman, do you accept perestroika in me?"

"Da!" I answered, nearly choking on a piece of nori.

"Well then," she beamed, "see you at the labor camp, comrade Romanoff!"

She giggled, kissed me again, and slammed the entrance door.

On the way to work, an exhausted Shmagy confirmed that my problem was solved.

"I'd like to note that I didn't even warm up," he said. "I don't want to make that confused girl dependent on me."

His face stretched in a blissful smile, and his eyes got wet with tears of happiness, "I'm Shmagy. I'm a drug."

No, Thank You

I WAS SURPRISED by how quickly I got accepted by the team.

Jessica, who was interested in Shmagy's true talent, took me under her wing and stopped bugging me about my non-existent US passport. She also educated me on the rules inside American companies. For example, a sex-related joke can earn you a complaint about sexual harassment. It doesn't matter whether you mean it or if you are plain stupid or some combination thereof. Your ass will get fired.

"So, Roman, let's keep the best stuff away from Embarcadero Road," Jessica said as she winked at me, casting a look around and searching for Shmagy.

My colleague, Vadim, gave me the best advice about pronunciation.

"You, Roman," he said, "have the same crooked tongue like myself. We can never speak without a Russian accent. That's why we must forget throat sounds and speak English just like we speak Russian. This is called identity. They'll fire anybody who berates it. So, just relax and keep hurting their ears."

My manager, Prashant, and I walked once a week among the swamps, discussing technical things, and every time, Prashant tried to push me into full-time employment.

"Roman," he would say, "I'll give you a ton of stock options, full medical and paid vacation. You'll become a part of the family!"

"Thank you, Prashant," I would answer. "I don't believe in stock options, my medical is excellent, and I already have a family."

I believed in stock options, I didn't have any medical and my family was far, far away.

Settling Up

Soon, I paid off my debts and thought about moving out, but Shmagy stopped me.

"If you live alone," he said, "you have to pay out several times more, and what's the point? Bring chicks here. They dig this place. It gets them puzzled because they've never seen such a dump."

I agreed to stay, but changes would have to be made. First of all, I decided to replace the yoga mat with a brand new bed from IKEA.

On the way home from IKEA, we managed to hit a Toyota Corolla from the back, and the box with my bed slid off from the roof of Shmagy's car, breaking the rear window of the Toyota. The Toyota driver was reduced to tears, saying that she had no insurance or money to repair it. Shmagy decided that I needed a car and summoned all of his charisma to get me a good discount.

When we arrived at the DMV to register the car sale, they asked for my social security number and driver's license. I didn't have either, so I applied for a SSN, took a written test for a driver's license, scheduled a practical driving exam and in two weeks, had both my SSN and my driver's license.

After I received both cards by mail, I went to the bank to open my personal checking account. The clerk asked me if I wanted to apply for a credit card. I agreed and was approved on the spot.

Who could have known that my simple desire to move from the floor to a normal bed would put into motion all of those gears? But since I'd joined NN Inc., things seemed to start working for me.

I hoped to become a real somebody and show everyone back home that I was worthy.

But most of all, I wanted to prove myself to Julie.

Termination of Jessica

O NE DAY, Prashant called all the engineers in the conference room and announced that we had been rewarded with a boat trip in San Francisco Bay. I said a firm "No" but Prashant, who had laughed like a hyena when Shmagy had told him a story about a race to Farallon Islands, assured me that it was OK and no trouble awaited me in the Bay.

On Friday morning, we arrived at Pier 5 in San Francisco and embarked on the boat. First, we rounded Alcatraz and then set course to Angel Island for a BBQ.

NN, Inc. paid for the drinks, and we all took advantage of that opportunity to relax after many long hours in the office. Shmagy and I were experienced alcoholics, but most of the team were teetotalers. Too many Margaritas consumed too fast made our comrades open and talkative.

Ramesh, our Python programmer, told us about all the sacrifices his Indian family had had to make to educate him and buy him an airline ticket to the States.

Leighton, the database admin, talked about the merciless pressure that Chinese parents put on their children.

"You know who I hate most of all?" he asked. "Mozart! I spent seven years in music school, and I hope that I never touch a piano again!"

...

The happiest person on the boat was Portia. She had recently been promoted to executive assistant of our CEO, and this boat trip was her idea.

She sat next to Leighton, and after he had finished his piano story, everybody looked at her.

Portia smiled and said, "I just want to listen."

I wasn't surprised. Portia never talked about herself in public.

"You know, Roman," she'd once told me, "I am probably more of a foreigner in America than you are. Whatever I overcame, whatever I achieved, Jessicas would always come and say, 'She just got lucky' or 'It's because she's black'."

She did have a point. Her promotion was well-deserved, but jealous Jessica kept whining around the office, "If I was black, I'd be promoted too."

So Portia just sat there, enjoying and not sharing.

...

Jessica wasn't enjoying it at all. She was yawning and looking around as if we were not proper people to hang out with. When she told us that America was only for true Americans, Shmagy, obviously irritated, asked her to go with him to the front of the boat. Soon, he called me. I took a bottle of whiskey from the bar and joined them.

...

We sat on the deck, hanging our legs overboard and watching how the sun played on the ripples of the Bay and how the Golden Gate Bridge would dissolve in the clouds off Farallon islands, only to reappear moments later in all its glory.

We passed the bottle around, and every drink would make the golden gleam under our feet softer and softer and raise our moods higher and higher.

A fresh wind was blowing into our faces—the

same wind of hope that made me fall in love with San Francisco the first day we met. It was my place to be. We needed each other. The City of poets and vagabonds had accepted me.

...

Somebody approached us from behind. We turned our heads and saw Portia.

Jessica wasn't happy.

"What do you want here?" Jessica asked. "Did we bother you?"

"I'm a free gal," replied Portia. "I can chill wherever I want."

"Chill in the back, will ya?" Jessica responded in a melodic Southern accent and added, "Exactly where you belong, Miss executive assistant."

"Whatcha mean, bitch?"

"I ain't mean nothing, bitch," Jessica replied, imitating Portia's ebonic speech. "Just let me be, OK?"

"Hey, Karen," Portia quickly retorted, "check your privilege. Not too heavy for your pale shoulders, is it?"

"My privilege?" a visibly frustrated Jessica challenged. "My ancestors came here on the Mayflower. I'm a true American and I ended up checking green cards and handing paychecks to people who cannot even speak fucking English. My entire fortune is an old Honda Civic and twenty thousand dollars in student loan debt. That's my fucking privilege, and I can share it with you if you want."

"Poor baby," smirked Portia. "Your ancestors came here as free people, and mine were transported in ship holds like cattle."

"I'm a person, just like you or them!"—she continued as she pointed to Shmagy and me—"But when people see me, they think that I'm supposed to rap, or smoke crack, or shoot somebody or whatever. You have no fucking idea how I feel."

"That's nonsense," replied Jessica. "What're ya smoking? Be decent and nobody will think that of you. Why the fuck did you come here? We don't want you."

And so on and so forth it went.

Shmagy and I didn't even interfere. We just sat there, with dropped jaws, amazed how fast and ugly things had escalated.

Soon, Jessica had lost it completely, screaming, "Fuck you!" accompanied by the n-word.

Portia didn't say anything. Instead, she reached for her cell phone as she walked away.

By the time Jessica had stepped on Angel Island, she had already been fired.

...

I left NN, Inc. within a week because Jessica's replacement, Amy, threatened to call immigration if I didn't produce my green card.

To help me again, Shmagy tried to apply his bulletproof method. He touched Amy's hand and gazed into her eyes like they were filled with treasure. But Amy wasn't Jessica, and Shmagy's shenanigans almost got him fired for sexual harassment.

"I... I just looked at her," Shmagy complained as we drove home. "And she is like, 'It's uncalled for. It's inappropriate.'

"Tell me, my friend, how to live in this ruthless world?" he asked me, devastated by the system failure.

Without Work

I DID EXPECT that, sooner or later, I might leave NN, Inc., because the corp-to-corp option works for undocumented folks only if HR doesn't know her duties or neglects them.

Fortunately, I had several thousand dollars in the bank. I could sell my car for another eight, and I had a credit card. So, I could survive for at least six months.

I was also happy to stay at home because I'd recently started my own project.

Here is how it happened.

Shmagy made a video of my misery during the race to Farallon Islands and wanted to share it with our friends. But 18 megabytes was too much to send by email, and there was no way to post a video on the web directly from a cell phone. We brainstormed and decided to make an engine to upload video files from a cell phone and convert them into the Flash format. That way, users could watch those videos on their web browsers from both desktop computers and mobile devices.

...

The first video we converted and watched was the one from the ocean race.

The video quality was awful. The ocean, sailboat and my exhausted body were hardly recognizable in moving blocks of pixels. But the sound was excellent. Everyone who watched the video couldn't help but smile, hearing my vomiting, swearing and groans.

Jessica, who stopped by our Fulton apartment, giggled her heart out and asked me to send her a link to the video so she could share with girls from the theatre.

"What theatre?" Shmagy asked her in confusion.

"Fletcher Brothers Theatre on O'Farrell street," she replied. "It's not exactly a theatre. It's more like a strip club."

Jessica got a gig at the "theatre" the day after

being exiled from NN, Inc.

"So, how is it?" Shmagy asked her with sincere interest.

"Less money, more ugly mugs and the same grief." She tried to look upset, but her eyes were smiling at us.

I knew that I only had a few seconds before Jessica and Shmagy got busy.

"I'll work on video quality and send you a link," I promised her.

"I cannot wait!" she said as she sent me a 'mwah' through the air and disappeared into Shmagy's quarters.

Knives

I SOON REALIZED that my money wouldn't last as long as I had hoped. I had the wrong idea that, after you've earned money, it's yours. But the corporate tax, car registration fees and payments to the lawyer and accountant proved me wrong, sucking out a good portion from my checking account.

To stretch my budget, I bought a sack of rice and a sack of beans and decided to eat them instead of takeouts. Shmagy forecasted that I'd endure no longer than a week.

He was wrong. I gave up in three days.

Those three days, I was choking on tasteless black and white pulp and so starved that my legs ran for a burger and fries, ignoring my iron will.

"Attaboy!" praised Shmagy. "It's better to kill yourself than to live on rice and beans!"

To make sure that I wouldn't restart my saving experiments, he took both sacks to the ever-starving exchange students who lived on the third floor.

I heard roaring applause before a blushing Shmagy came back down.

"There are two kinds of people, Roman," he said. "Earners and savers. You are not a saver, but you can earn. So earn."

"Like I don't want to," I replied.

"You need to meet Igor!"

Igor came from a small town in Siberia. His father, a professional criminal, had taught him how to craft traditional thug knives, which Igor was making at his tiny workshop in Daly City.

His knives did look amazing. The narrow blades were shiny and sharp, and the stacked multi-colored handles echoed the stained-glass windows of Notre-Dame de Paris.

Igor was happy to make me his business partner

because he wanted to try a new selling technique and needed someone to share the shame.

To execute his plan, Igor recycled the cardboard left from my IKEA bed and made two large display cases with wired loops to hold knives. Each display case was hung on the neck with a dog collar and completely covered the chest and belly of its bearer.

Looking like two organ grinders, we went from house to house in Mountain View and Palo Alto, knocking on the doors and trying to sell directly to customers.

At first, the potential customers looked on in bewilderment at two awkward guys in dog collars who mumbled something with a Russian accent, pointing to the shitload of multi-colored knives on their chests.

But, alas, it was obvious that our merchandise had only one practical usage—to stab somebody.

"Good luck with that," the potential customers would tell us before shutting their doors and releasing their furious pugs to their tiny backyards.

We spent a week on the streets and made just one sale. More precisely, it was an exchange. One little girl offered us a plush monkey for the big, mean knife that she really liked. Her supportive father approved the deal and called the cops.

When the cop saw us and heard our accent, he was so touched by our misery that he didn't fine us for conducting business without a license. Moreover, he suggested we try selling the knives online.

That was a good idea. I created an online store with WordPress, we purchased online ads and the knives started to sell.

I was also working on my own project. Soon, the picture quality in my video upload project had improved and I could finally email Jessica a link to the ocean race video.

Kevin

SEVERAL WEEKS PASSED, and there was still no reply from Jessica.

One Saturday morning, Shmagy looked through the window and exclaimed with awe, "That's what I call a ride!"

Somebody banged on the door with her foot, I opened it, and there came Jessica—embracing some guy we didn't know.

Jessica was drinking champagne from a bottle, and her companion carried a gift basket with crackers, cheese, olives and other assorted bits.

"This is Kevin!" Jessica exclaimed. "Say *Hi*, kids!"

"Hi, Kevin!"

We shook hands and ran outside to check out the ride. And, indeed, it was a ride to be checked—a legendary McLaren F1.

Shmagy circled around the McLaren, smacking his lips and savoring every detail of the beast. He even got behind the steering wheel and honked the horn. I was sure that he would have kissed the car had he been alone.

We went inside and started to terminate the goodies from the gift basket.

"So, what do you, guys, do?" Kevin asked.

"Well," Shmagy answered, "we code and also do our own projects. What about yourself?"

"I work for Cipres Capital," Kevin responded proudly. "Have you heard about venture capital?"

"Yep!"

"Roman, show him your vomit video!" Jessica suggested and, at that very moment, Kevin's phone ranged.

Kevin apologized and left, but after several minutes, he called Jessica and invited the three of us to his birthday party the next day.

"Where did you dig up such a treasure?" Shmagy asked Jessica.

"What do you mean *where*? At work, of course!"

she winked.

"Come here, you skank," Shmagy said with tenderness and took her to his room.

At Kevin's Party

KEVIN lived just a few minutes off freeway 280, in a small village called Los Altos Hills. The cheapest house in that village cost three million dollars. It definitely was not farmers who lived there.

Kevin was happy to see us and introduced our trinity as his crazy Russian friends, including true American Jessica.

At an American party, you wander from one group to another, trying to impress strangers by talking to them about nothing. I didn't want to shock innocent people with my terrible accent and had no idea where to put myself. An attentive Kevin took notice and invited me for a walk with his black lab, Bailey.

We went strolling on the crooked streets, hidden among old pines and redwoods. I was looking at unpretentious California-style houses made out of plywood and fake stones, and couldn't understand why people paid millions for what reminded me of oversized chicken coops.

Kevin interrupted my frustration.

"You know, Roman, I have more millions than

this tree has limes," Kevin said, pointing at a lemon tree bent under the weight of countless fruits.

"But whatever fortune you accumulate, one day you'll realize the value of simple things like a talk with a friend, a juicy steak or a fat joint."

"Or a million-dollar McLaren," I continued his list.

"Haha!" he responded. "Do you want to take a ride?"

"Ask!"

"Where do you wanna go?" he asked. "Maybe to Palo Alto? Let's make them snooty chicks on University Avenue drop their jaws!"

Wreck on Sand Hill Road

A S WE RODE, Kevin told me about his studies at Stanford, his startups and other *simple things*.

Just like me, Kevin used to be a programmer, and he made his first big money selling his internet company to eBay.

It was strange to hear that a regular person could make a fortune without theft or high connections, the most common ways to get rich in Russia.

We drove on Sand Hill Road, a street that had more VC companies than Igor had unsold knives.

I started to record the video on my cell phone, first capturing the street and then filming the inside of the car. Then, for no reason, I asked Kevin, "So what can this do?"

Kevin smiled, and a mischievous spark flashed in his eyes as he replied, "Watch this!"

First, he pressed the pedal to the floor and then sharply turned the steering wheel to the left, trying to change lanes.

We began spinning, then we hit the curb, rolled over in the air and crashed into an electric pole.

As I was whispering goodbye to my life, the Mc-

Laren landed on its roof with a raucous metallic groan.

For a few seconds, we just sat there upside down, not believing that we had survived.

Kevin took his sweaty palms off the steering wheel, looked at them, and said in a disconnected manner,

"Happy birthday, bitch!"

A Chance

FORTUNATELY, we hadn't hit any other cars. After the police and ambulance did their part, we called a tow truck and rode back to Kevin's house in it.

The mutilated McLaren was unloaded onto the lawn while Kevin and I went on to drink hard liquor to celebrate our survival. As it turned out, Kevin had bought the car just a week ago, and it was his first car with a stick shift and superpower.

Jessica joined us. She hugged Kevin, called him her pumpkin, and, of course, produced that signature American sound of fake compassion,

"Awwww!"

Kevin's elderly maid, Tía Juana, kept praying and looking at him with love and concern. *Loco, pero amable* (crazy but kind) was how she described her boss. When she got ahold of herself, she brought us tacos so we wouldn't get too drunk too fast.

Then I remembered the video that I had started to record right before the wreck. I got everything, including Kevin's "Happy birthday, bitch!"

A million-dollar car was now totaled, and we'd almost met the Lord just a couple of hours ago. But that phrase was so funny that we played it over and over again on my old Nokia. Kevin's guests joined us, and they too appreciated the tragicomedy.

"We need to show this video to the boss," one of Kevin's colleagues said.

"Only if we send the file by email," Kevin answered.

"We can do it without email!" I exclaimed, remembering my project. "We can use Flash."

Kevin almost jumped.

"You said Flash?"

"Yes," I replied. "I've been working on a video converter for several months now."

Kevin took me to his home office, gave me a MacBook Pro and said, "Kick ass, man. It's your chance!"

The Fate of One Birdie

MY HEART was throbbing so hard that I could hear it. Here it was, my big chance! I could show my software to the whole bunch of Silicon Valley VCs. It was the ultimate, unreal luck!

I copied a video file from my phone to the hard drive, uploaded it to my test server, and launched the converter. After several minutes, the converter crashed. With shaky fingers, I opened a log file, analyzed the error message, and tried to fix the bug. But, by accident, I removed a good chunk of the Python code. I recovered the code from GIT, and tried to fix the bug once again. I then launched the converter to test the fix, but the system crashed just like before.

Kevin entered the room, and I turned my distraught face to him.

"You OK, man?" he asked.

It was a rhetorical question, however, as every atom of my body was so not fucking OK.

"Kevin," I said, "there is a bug. I cannot fix it."

"That's cool," he quipped. "Tomorrow I'm flying to Tokyo, so call me in a couple of weeks."

I went outside. Almost all of the guests had already left. Shmagy was chilling by the pool on the recliner, petting Kevin's cat.

"Let's go, man," I said, not recognizing my voice.

"Let's go," Shmagy replied and shouted, "Jessica!"

Jessica, sipping her tenth margarita, was balancing at the edge of the pool, trying to touch the water with her foot.

"I'm going to Japan with Kevin," she mumbled. "Leave me alone." She waved goodbye to Shmagy.

Shmagy approached her slowly, held her arm so she wouldn't fall and looked into her eyes with an unwinking stare.

"My kitty," he said, "let's go home. I'm going to tell you a sad story about the fate of a birdie."

Hypnotized, Jessica asked him in a weak voice, "What birdie?"

"The one who flew from one nest to another."

Shmagy put his birdie into the back seat of his car, and we took off for home.

The Root Cause

WE DROVE on freeway 280 to San Francisco in silence until I said, "Shmagy, it looks like I fucked up the best chance of my life."

"What happened?" he asked.

"I couldn't convert the freaking file," I replied in frustration. "I've converted hundreds of files from my phone. It used to work."

"What's the error message?"

...

When we arrived at Fulton, we sat in front of our laptops until we figured out the issue. One of the third-party libraries that I'd used to convert video files had a setting for a source file limit. The limit was 20 megabytes, but my file was 23. It was a simple fix to make, just a quick edit in the configuration file. But the error message stated "11136 - input file format error", which pointed in a completely different direction. We changed the settings to 30 megabytes and my video was converted on the spot. It was possible to watch my video via a web browser anywhere in the world!

Although it was around 2:00 am, I decided to call Kevin. Shmagy told me that it was better to send a link to the video via email, so I did.

That night, I was unable to sleep, waiting for Kevin's reply, which would never arrive.

Valleycrunch

IN THE MORNING, I wandered into the kitchen, made a cup of tea and as usual, checked the Valleycrunch, a popular tech blog about Silicon Valley.

On the first page, I saw Kevin's photo and an article titled *Star Silicon Valley VC in a Coma After a Car Crash*. Underneath the headline, I read that Kevin had crashed his Mercedes against a brick wall on freeway 280, speeding on a wet road. He was in a coma in the intensive care unit and his chances were thin.

Jessica came out of the shower in an oversized shirt she'd borrowed from Shmagy and a turban on her head made out of a white towel.

"That's it. I'll never drink again," she promised, wrinkling her face in pain from a hangover.

I put my laptop with the Valleycrunch article in front of her. She became pale and sank into the chair.

Then came Shmagy.

"Oh…" he said. "You already know."

Jessica fell to her knees, embracing Shmagy's legs and sobbing, "Oh my gosh, oh my gosh, oh my gosh."

Shmagy went to his room and returned with a 4.5-liter bottle of vodka that he'd been saving for his birthday.

"Nobody leaves this house today," he said, mopping tears from Jessica's face.

Bridge in the Fog

THE NEXT DAY, Jessica was dying from a hangover, just like the day before.

"From rags to riches and quickly back. A-fucking-mazing!" she sighed, staring at moldy kitchen ceilings and slurping pho that Shmagy had gotten to heal her.

They decided to take their minds off things and go to Napa Valley to visit the hot springs and wineries. They invited me, but I felt like staying home.

I. HAD. NO. IDEA. WHAT. TO. DO. NEXT.

Of course, I cared about Kevin, but I didn't know him well. I was more concerned about myself and was drowning in self pity, just like Jessica.

Just two days prior, I'd had my chance, some unexpected luck that could have changed my life and gotten me out of misery. But like always, things only got worse, and I hated myself for another failure.

I couldn't work in America. I couldn't go back to Russia. My money was almost gone. I wished I could cry, but I was falling into an abyss of despair and felt too empty and exhausted.

For no apparent reason, I hopped in my car and

drove to the Golden Gate Bridge.

The thick fog had already set in and a sticky, breathless cold had replaced the happy wind of hope. Suddenly, the horn from a barge passing below made a loud, long signal. She was just like me, wandering alone in the far seas and calling out to somebody in the fog. But unlike me, she was a useful thing.

I put my arms on the railings and leaned forward, looking down as if I wanted to see the barge.

My legs were already in the air when somebody laughed nearby. I pushed against the railings and got back on my feet. At that moment, two lovers came out of the fog. The girl tried to light a cigarette, but her fingers were so cold, she couldn't strike a match. I helped her.

"That's just perfect," she said. "We have a day in Sanfran, but the only thing you can see, I mean smell, is stinky seals on Pier 39. Ha ha ha!"

They both looked cold but happy and in love. She was wearing his jacket, and he was trying to warm her lilac hands in his palms.

"Guys," I said to them, "to hell with sightseeing. All you need is love."

We nodded at each other, and I went home.

Suddenly

From: Mark Hortman

To: Roman Monin

Subject: Fwd: Link to Happy Birthday Bitch video

Hi Roman,

I'm a general partner of Cipres Capital and Kevin's boss. According to the rules of the firm, I have access to his email.

I saw the video and would like to talk to you. I was hoping we could meet tomorrow at 5:00 pm at Cipres Capital office on Sand Hill Road.

Hope to see you then,

Mark

Changing the World One Black Square at a Time

IARRIVED at the Cipres Capital office at 4:50 pm. At 5.00 pm, Mark got off work, and we went to Moondance restaurant in Palo Alto.

Mark ordered us prime rib steaks and a bottle of cabernet from Napa. When I realized that the dinner would cost us 300 dollars, I became visibly upset. Mark calmed me down, saying that Silicon Valley VCs always pay for dinners when meeting potential founders.

"It's a local tradition, you know," he said.

We talked not only about my video converter but also about life in general. Mark listened with interest and directed our conversation to the things he wanted to know. He was trying to evaluate if he could trust me.

To my relief, he was fine with the fact that I didn't have employment authorization.

"The main thing is that your guest visa is current," he told me. "A work visa is not a problem if you have my lawyers."

After the dinner, we crossed El Camino Real and

went on for a walk at the Stanford campus.

Mark asked me how I'd come up with the video project I was working on.

"I don't know," I said. "I got sick on a boat and then one thing led to another."

Mark looked at me in a fatherly fashion.

"Let me tell you something about the Valley," he continued. "There is only one right answer to this question, and it is *I want to change the world.*"

"Of course, everybody wants to get rich, everyone is pushed by ego, ambition and personal things like an itch to prove something to a high school sweetheart who left him for some hairy Chad. There are many hidden motivations, but the game has rules and the right answer is always *I want to change the world!*"

"Exactly the same hypocrisy as in Russia," I said.

"Well, call that whatever you want," he replied, "but as a financier and philanthropist, I approve that motto. Venture investing is a tough game, but when your fortune reaches eight or better nine figures, you start thinking about intangible things like karma and legacy."

"No offense, Mark," I answered, "but it's easy for you to talk about intangible things. You probably have enough money for ten comfortable lives. I don't. I'm sure that some money would help me a lot."

"You are correct," he said, "but let me tell you what happens in the end if your motivation is getting rich instead of changing the world."

"When you are broke," Mark continued, "you have the illusion that money can make all of your problems go away. It's natural to think this way, and I don't blame you. So let's assume that you've just made several million dollars. Do you know what happens after you buy a house in Los Altos Hills and a McLaren F1? Nothing good. Because man's true problems are rooted in his head and they will not go away, whatever fortune he accumulates, because true problems are not caused by a lack of money.

"Eventually, one guy is snorting coke at 6 am, another buys an apartment and stuffs it with Japanese sex dolls, a third seeks for enlightenment somewhere in Tibet, and so on.

"But it's different when you do something with a passion for changing the world. Then, your path is noble, and your fortune is not the purpose, but rather a tool to disrupt more things.

"My personal definition of happiness is this: *Change the world and make money along the way.* So yes, we are here to change the world."

As I listened, I realized that Mark had already decided to work with me. Any help from a powerful man like him could make a big difference.

"By the way," he continued, "your project has a great potential to change the world. But other people do similar things already."

"Thank you, Mark!" I exclaimed. "You know, the

main thing that I cannot figure out is how to make money with it."

He smiled.

"You are new in the Valley," he said. "So, let me tell you another important thing. Venture capital doesn't care if your business is profitable or not. The thing we care about is the WOW factor of your startup."

"I don't understand," I said. "I always thought that a business should be profitable. That's the purpose."

"Nope!" he replied. "Investors, including venture capitalists, make money when they sell a startup they invested in for a profit—or when it goes public and its shares rise. These things have nothing to do with the profitability of a startup itself. Many now-profitable companies, like Amazon, have been losing money for years. It's because they spend all revenues on expanding their business, or because their product or business model is too revolutionary for their time."

"Well," I said, "if a business loses money, it should go bankrupt. Correct?"

"Correct," he answered, "but if money is needed, a VC provides another round of financing."

"Understood. But why is the WOW factor so important?" I asked.

"Let me ask you this: are you familiar with the Black Square, a famous painting by Kazimir Malevich?"

"Of course! Everybody jokes about it," I remembered the painting with nothing else but a black square.

"They can joke all day long, but if this painting ever hits the market, there will be a line of billionaires willing to pay tens of millions for it. You know why?"

"No. Why?"

"Because Black Square has the ultimate WOW factor. Nobody understands what the heck it is, but you can sell it in a nanosecond because there will always be people who want to invest in that scale of WOW factor. Hence, don't worry about making money. Worry about making a cool product. The product with the WOW factor."

Mark smiled again, looking at my puzzled face.

"Roman," he said, "I cannot finance your project at this time. My business partners will not understand. But I'm still going to give you a chance. In one month, I want to see a working prototype where users can register, upload video and watch it on both cell phones and desktop computers."

"Thank you, Mark!" I said. "I'll do my best. And thanks for the dinner, the talk and your trust."

"My pleasure, Roman! It's up to you now."

A Second Chance

I CALLED SHMAGY from the road, and he told me he was in. When I came home, he had already attached a large whiteboard to the wall in the kitchen. He had borrowed it from the third-floor students who regarded him as a demigod after giving them my rice and beans.

We started brainstorming.

Who did what? What should we code first—front end or back end? Did we need a dedicated server or shared account? What software to use for a database? What features were essential? Should we get help with web design and testing? And so on and so forth it went.

We kept filling up the whiteboard, adding, changing or removing things. To capture our ideas, flowcharts and mockups, we took photos of the whiteboard and saved them in Evernote.

We only got to our beds in the early morning hours, exhausted but happy.

Later that day, Shmagy wrote an email to Prashant with a heartbreaking message that Shmagy's favorite uncle had been mauled by his pet brown bear and was waiting on his deathbed for his favorite nephew. Prashant gave Shmagy a month of unpaid vacation. It was great news because Shmagy was a more experienced developer than myself.

For starters, I had to tune up my video conversion engine and then switch to the front end. I was also in charge of integration, end-to-end and cross-device testing. Shmagy was responsible for database and infrastructure, like version control and a bug-tracking system.

We decided to support the first version of the iPhone that was just released. It had a huge WOW factor, in spite of lacking many standard features of Nokia.

We soon realized that, due to the complete absence of artistic taste, I'd been crafting anything BUT a nice user interface. Rather, it was a Frankenstein made of bright colors, an ugly logo, strange font types and confusing object alignment.

Shmagy suggested we include Igor in our team because he could draw and even mastered Photoshop to design new knives.

To our surprise, we did everything right. Everyone knew what they were doing and what the others were doing, and our progress was obvious.

A generous Shmagy was buying us pizza and beer every evening because Igor and I were in such bad financial shape. I'd started to write down Shmagy's expenses in the hopes of paying him back one day, but he found the paper with my records and burnt it right in front of me, "Eat, drink, code, and don't fuck my brain, alrighty?"

Alas, pizza and beer weren't enough to survive, so I had to sell my old faithful Toyota. I had only used it to drive to the Bridge, but I figured that a 30-minute run would get me there anyway.

Dot Love

IT WAS TIME to name our startup. As usual, we brainstormed and came up with many ideas. At some point, I suggested, "What about *Dot Love*? It's about love, and it sounds Internet-like."

Everybody agreed, and Jessica even proclaimed,

> *"Dot love, or not dot love, that's the question!*
> *Whether 'tis nobler in the mind*
> *To be a princess of the dump,*
> *Or a maid in the mansion?"*

Once we had decided on a company name, we registered the domain name and changed the DNS settings to point to our server.

Now we had to develop and test on live environment. That didn't matter yet because nobody knew the URL to our frontpage except the domain registrar and us.

I had never enjoyed my work so much! Everyone in our close-knit crew felt a fair wind, a touch of luck and a powerful wave taking us forward.

Yes, we had tons of bugs and limitations, but our

software was a huge step forward from my initial video converter. Our user interface was clean and intuitive. Our back end was fast and well-written. Our infrastructure allowed continuous integration, quick release to production and, if needed, a pain-less rollback.

At times, we had a weird feeling that the project itself was helping us to complete it. It felt like we were connected to some magic source from where we could scoop ideas, solutions and even stamina.

One day, Igor smoked some potent Sativa grown by our friend Petrovich and had an insight.

"Dot Love is like a book," he told us. "It's not us who write it. It writes itself, using us. I can't com-plain!"

"Igor!" Shmagy yelled from his room. "So, where is the logo j-fucking-peg?"

"First git fetch, then git checkout, then 'I'm sor-ry,'" Igor replied.

"Sorry for what?" Shmagy asked him.

"You discombobulated the straightforwardness of my intellectualization!"

It was a good Sativa.

...

Just as Mark had advised me, we developed a functional prototype with four main features: Reg-istration, Login, Video upload and Video playback.

It wasn't clear what to do next. For example, a

user posts a video, someone watches it, then what?

We'd built a solid foundation but had no idea what to erect on it.

In any case, the job was done.

We were ready to see Mark.

What's the Plan, Mr. Shmagy?

I EMAILED MARK, but he didn't reply. After a week had passed, I emailed again and got a response from his assistant saying Mark was busy and he would get back to me once things settled down.

I showed the assistant's email to my colleagues.

"Fuck that shit!" exclaimed Shmagy.

Igor slapped his palm on the kitchen table and started to stab at the spaces between fingers with his razor-sharp knife. He struck with such anger that one wrong move would chop off his finger like a piece of cucumber. 1-2-1-3-1-4-1-5-1-6, the knife was bruising the table, but no one cared.

I also got mad. It was clear that Mark had fucked us up.

"No way I'm gonna give up!" I proclaimed. "What's his phone number?"

We called Jessica, who, thanks to the "theater" and Kevin, had established many useful connections in the world of venture capital. Jessica told us that Mark was celebrating his daughter's birthday at the Jack London Park in Glen Ellen.

It was about a two-hour drive.

We hopped into Shmagy's Lexus and took off without further discussions.

After we passed the Golden Gate Bridge and a tunnel, Igor asked, "So, what's the plan?"

Shmagy pulled over and replied, "Yes, what's the plan?"

At that exact moment, a CHP cruiser stopped behind us, and a cop approached the driver's side.

"Is there a problem?" the officer asked.

Shmagy looked at him with grave desperation and replied, "Yes, there is a problem. The problem is that some fuckers don't keep their promises!"

"That's not a reason to stop on the freeway," the cop informed him. "Your driver's license, please."

It was all too much for poor Shmagy. He closed the window and released such a ferocious cascade of swears, curses and roars that the car almost exploded into millions of particles.

Meanwhile, the cop called for backup, and within moments, he was joined by two more patrol cruisers.

Cops pointed guns in our direction and asked us to step out of the car.

After they had checked the documents and tested Shmagy's breath for alcohol, they lectured him on his manners and gave him a ticket.

When we continued our way to Glen Ellen, Igor mentioned that it was better to have no plan than to have a plan that would land us all in jail because of Shmagy's temper.

Shmagy asked Igor to shut the fuck up or he would really lose it.

There was no more talking.

Getting to Know Sofia

JUST OUTSIDE of Glen Ellen, we saw an SUV parked askew on the side of the road and a couple arguing about something.

Suddenly, the guy pushed the girl so hard that she almost fell on her back.

Shmagy hit the brakes, backed up the car and jumped out.

After a brief exchange of what-the-fuck, fuck-you, fuck-you-too, the guy took off into the air and landed in a thicket of poison oak. Shmagy wanted to continue, but we stopped him.

The guy hopped into his car, wished us all to die young and drove away. The girl remained behind.

When she had calmed down, she told us that he was her possessive boyfriend. It was her birthday, but they had to leave the party early because he had gotten mad, thinking that a young partner from her dad's firm was flirting with her.

As a flashback, I remembered Julie's wannabe boyfriend, Parigin, who'd almost landed me in prison.

"What's your dad's name?" Shmagy asked her.

"Mark Hortman."

"And your name is?"

"Sofia Hortman."

"By the way," Shmagy chirped, "we are going to your birthday party."

"Ha!" Sofia retorted. "You can go wherever you want, but I'm not going back."

"What about Sonoma?"

"Okey-dokey," she replied.

It was a short drive to downtown Sonoma, and we parked right in front of the old Catholic mission. First, we wanted to visit local wineries, but Igor snubbed us, saying that business comes first and we could always get wasted at home. We agreed with his reasoning and found a coffee shop just around the corner.

Sofia soon surrendered to Shmagy's charms and felt relaxed and comfortable. She put her head of golden curls on his shoulder and sipped her milkshake with a wide smile on her pretty face.

"Shmagy, I feel so secure," she cooed. "You are a true gentleman."

"It's because you, my curly Sue, are a true lady," he replied.

"It's because you, my Tarzan, are a true gentleman," Sofia flirted back.

Shmagy's hand was already squeezing Sofia's buttocks—left, right, left, right—as if he was checking the ripeness of a cantaloupe.

I realized that it was time to act or they would leave the rest of us behind. Shmagy had already stretched his neck, looking for a hotel.

"Sofia," I asked, "is your father still at the party?"

"Yep," she responded. "He is buttering up some devs who convert mobile videos so they can be viewed in a web browser. He invited them to my birthday party to show how much he cared, haha. He..."

"Wait!" I interrupted her. "This is our project! It was our idea!"

"I don't know," she replied. "It's different people."

It was Shmagy's turn to freak out.

"What do you mean, *it's different people*?" he demanded. "Roman, get your laptop. Show her!"

I opened Dot Love website and showed her two test videos.

"Not bad!" she said. "By the way, I made a video at the party. You wanna watch?"

"No!" Shmagy retorted. "We don't wanna watch. Fuck that party, and fuck your sweet dad. That's it. I'm going home."

He stood up and gulped up his coffee.

"Shmagy, wait!" Igor exclaimed. "Sofia, listen. Do you want to try to upload your video to our site?"

"Why should I?" she asked.

"You can send a short URL to your friends," answered Igor. "Also, please show it to your dad and tell him that we don't need business partners like him."

"Okey-dokey, but let him..."—she pointed at Shmagy—"be a gentleman again."

We all cast an evil eye at Shmagy and he gave up.

"Fine," he huffed. "Let me introduce myself. My name is Shmagy. I'm a gentleman."

I took Sofia's iPhone and uploaded the latest file from her library to our server. After several minutes, I received an email confirming successful conversion and emailed Sofia a link to her video.

"Let's watch it on your laptop," she said to me.

I started the video. It began normally enough. People stood in groups, talking, drinking and laughing. Then, the video showed lush vineyards, and the camera closed in on Jack London's cottage. We saw two men standing on the doorstep. One man was Mark Hortman, and the other was... Hugh.

The same Hugh who'd almost fed us to the sharks after trying to set up a spinnaker near the Farallon Islands.

"Shmagy, how long have you known that Hugh?" I asked my dear friend, whose face was becoming as red as a ripe tomato.

"Long enough!" Shmagy fumed. "He used to work at NN, Inc. I sent him the first version of our video and asked for his feedback."

Sofia added insult to injury.

"That's their team lead!" she quipped. "He showed us a funny video where some Russian guy was puking like a whale."

"That Russian guy is me," I said.

"And I'm that angry guy who is going to drive there and kill that fucking Hugh," barked Shmagy, clearly out of gentleman mode.

"Shmagy," I interrupted, "but how could Hugh find out about our technology?"

"Well, he is a top programmer," he replied. "I always ask him when I have a question."

"So, they just stole our technology and got ahead of us?"

I didn't need an answer. Things had become quite clear.

"By the way," Sofia interjected, "your software is way better than theirs. Conversion is quick, URL is short, video quality is superb! Let me email it to my dad. Let him suffer, haha."

Shmagy looked at her in anger.

"I'll make sure of that," he said. "I am gonna send this video to all the ventures in the Valley with the subject: *Please get acquainted with a thief, a fucker and a bastard, Mark Hortman*. I'm gonna..."

"And you'll make a fool of yourself!" interrupted Sofia. "Don't take it personally! That's just how the game is played. I'm sending him a link right now."

There came an uncomfortable pause, and Shmagy asked her, "Can we give you a lift?"

"No, it's OK."

"Bye then!" he called out.

"Wait, you crazy Russians. I have a gift for you."

Sofia opened her Louis Vuitton bag and took out an old book with a blue cover.

"Dad sponsors the Jack London Park and they gave him this," she said. "It's Martin Eden, a special edition published in 1911."

I snatched the book, put it against my chest, and gave my friends a mean stare.

"It's mine. Okey-dokey?"

...

Our trio returned to Fulton.

Igor went home. Shmagy and I dispersed to our rooms without a word.

In the evening, my Moscow friend, Paust, called me and said that Parigin had come to his senses. His and Julie's families were friends, just like before, and their parents had pressured them to marry.

"When it rains, it pours," I thought to myself as I poured a full glass of whiskey.

I was about to toast to all losers and fuckwits when somebody banged on the door with her foot. I opened and out of the fog came Jessica, Sofia, Mark and Hugh.

All the World's a Stage

MARK RUSHED FORWARD, hugged me, and sang, "Oh, Rommy boy, oh Rommy boy! You got it wrong."

I gently pushed him away and answered, "Explain then, so Rommy boy gets it right."

"Hugh has developed a set of algorithms for a relevant search using file metadata and patterns of user behavior," he explained. "Let me give you an example. When you search for Hotel California, you'll also get Desperado because it's an Eagles song and Stairway to Heaven because it's also classic rock. Do you follow?"

"Yes," I said, "I do. I just don't understand if you are still interested in us."

"Of course, I am! I just wanted to talk to Hugh before talking to you," Mark smiled at me as if it was obvious. "See, you make me talk in rhymes."

I was gazing at him, puzzled and in disbelief.

"Come on!" he said. "Stop that bull and show me how far you got."

I demonstrated the end-to-end user flow and answered all his technical questions.

Impressed, Mark looked around at everybody and said, "Everybody in this room will become a multi."

I didn't understand. "A multi?"

"Yes, a multimillionaire," he replied.

Shmagy, all red like a steamed lobster, looked at Mark with hostility and said, "It's all bullshit. We are fed up with your promises. If you mean business, let's talk about figures, and all of it should be put into the contract. Otherwise, we're gonna talk to other people. They know about us in the Valley!"

Of course, nobody knew about us except Jessica and her colleagues from the strip club. But Shmagy sounded so convincing that even I believed him.

Mark, however, was also convincing.

"Do you know who I am?" he asked. "Do you think I'm joking here? Certainly, we'll sign a contract. We just need to distribute shares and figure out the evaluation of the company. I'll pay for my stake in cash to give you seed money."

Mark sighed as if preparing to bring us bad news.

"And Hugh will be your software architect," he said finally.

"What?" Shmagy exclaimed, jumping out of his skin. "It was us who did the project! We don't need Hugh!"

"You do and you will," Mark retorted. "You just don't understand. We are drowning in big data and at the same time, personalization is essential.

That's why personalized searches on large sets of data are a top priority. Hugh wrote his algorithms especially for that. Moreover, he has the whole codebase. You just need to integrate his code with yours and we are all set. Besides, Hugh can envision the whole distributed system. He is the best man for a job!"

I wasn't entirely swayed.

"We need to think about it," I told him. "We don't have big data. We don't even know what to do with our project. I have nothing against Hugh, but we need to understand why we need him and what stake we should give him."

"Give him five percent," Mark replied. "Then, thirty goes to you and your pal," he said as he pointed to Shmagy. "Five goes to your third guy, and thirty goes to a pool for future employees. Hence, mine is 30 percent. In fact, let's do this: I evaluate your company at 100K, so I'm paying 30K in cash for my shares."

He put his fingers to his forehead as if he had forgotten something.

"Roman," he said, "we've brought some food. Please, help me out."

When we got outside, Mark stopped me and asserted, "Hugh will be my man in the company. Otherwise, the deal is off."

His tone enraged me.

"Mark," I objected, "I don't understand what kind of a game you are playing. Sorry, but I don't really trust you anymore."

"Roman, do you realize what you are doing?" he asked.

"No, tell me, Mark."

"All the world's a stage," he replied, quoting the Bard, "and all the men and women merely players."

"So what?" I replied.

"So," he started, "I want to produce a nice play with you as the main character. And here is the plot: Hugh works for Dot Love, I provide advice and financing, Dot Love becomes a unicorn and you become filthy rich. So, is that OK or...?"

"OK," I answered. "But I want to see the contract."

We came back inside.

Shmagy was circling the kitchen, and I felt certain he was about to spoil it for all of us. I took him outside and told him, "If you hit anybody or do something stupid, you'll go to jail and nobody will ever finance Dot Love. Your choice."

Suddenly, his round face stretched in a dreamy smile.

"Did you get Sofia's number?" Shmagy asked, motioning his palms forward as if he was holding a watermelon. "I miss her, hmm, soul already."

He sniffed and tried to depict sadness.

"Damn man," I said. "You are a piece of work."

We hugged.

A Contract

THE NEXT DAY, we received a 200-page contract. Igor caved right away.

"Guys," he said, "you dig into it and just tell me where to sign."

We started to dig, each on his own computer.

Soon, Shmagy exclaimed, "Roman, check out page four. That stinky rat, Hugh, got more stocks behind our backs."

I checked and saw that Hugh had received ten percent instead of the previously promised five. Hence, the pool for future employees fell from thirty to twenty-five percent.

The proposed list of shareholders looked like this:

30% - Cipres Capital

25% - A pool for future employees

15% - Roman

15% - Shmagy

10% - Hugh

5% - Igor

But the good news was that Dot Love was evaluated at 500K instead of 100K. Thus, Cipres Capital would transfer to us 150K as soon as their lawyers registered the company and opened a bank account for us.

Igor, who heard our conversation, said, "I don't mind if Hugh gets 10 percent. The problem is that he will report to Mark about everything."

That made Shmagy jump.

"That's what was bugging me!" he barked. "That stupid fucker, Hugh, did a similar project. What if he steals our code?"

"But do we have a choice?" I asked him. "They are giving us 150K as seed money. And our investor is not a regular Joe like us. He's Mark freaking Hortman."

"Sure," grumbled Shmagy, "let's pretend that everything is just peachy. But let me tell you this: every time I see that fucking Hugh, he'll be reading a juicy 'Fuck you!' right in my eyes."

"It's a deal!" Igor and I exclaimed with relief.

Reverse Vesting

W<small>E CONTINUED</small> to read the contract, and we all shouted at the same time, "Wait a minute! What is that?"

According to the contract, Dot Love was going to issue 1,000,000 shares. That meant that Shmagy and I would get 150,000 shares each. But, it hinged on the condition of... what is *reverse vesting*?

We googled it and found out that we would have to work for Dot Love for five years to vest our shares. In other words, each of us would be rewarded 30,000 shares for each year of work.

So, if you stayed with the company for five years, you would be good to go. But if you decided to leave the company or, if you were fired for one of a million possible reasons, you would lose your unvested shares.

Jessica Comes to the Rescue

A VERY DISAPPOINTED SHMAGY rolled a joint and went outside. I called Jessica.

"Sista," I said, "come on over."

"Can't right now," she replied. "I'm in a meeting."

"But Shmagy is heartbroken," I told her. "Your tender friends from Sand Hill Road try to screw us hard every time we meet them."

"What's the problem now?"

"It's about reverse vesting," I explained.

Soon, I heard a man's slightly hoarse voice.

"Hi," he said. "This is Steve, here. So the question is about reverse vesting?"

"Hi Steve, I'm Roman," I answered. "Yes. They want to invest in our company and have stipulated five years of reverse vesting. Is that a trap?"

"Nope," he assured me, "it's quite normal. Get into a pair of VC shoes for a minute. Let's say you are a co-founder with a crapload of shares, and you want to leave the company, but still keep your shares to yourself. In other words, you want to do nothing for a company anymore but still own a chunk of it. Neither the investors nor the business itself would benefit from that."

I was trying to digest what I'd just heard.

"You probably think that the race is over once you release the new software and users flock to it?" Steve continued. "Sorry to disappoint you, but that's exactly where the race starts. And most runners will never make it to the finish line.

"Remember this: a typical startup is a sort of fuckery that, instead of a happy 'Oh!', usually ends up with the tears of people who lost their time and money."

"I got it, Steve," I said. "But is it possible to change that clause? I mean, reverse vesting?"

"Yes. But it depends on how firm they hold you by the balls."

"And how am I to determine that?" I wondered.

"Do you have just one interested investor?" he asked.

"Yes."

"Then your balls are in the VC's vice grip," he said. "I'm sorry, but not really. You need to understand something. There are thousands of wannabes like you in the Valley. People wait a year to pitch something to me. Even if you're a genius and your product is truly a gem, there is no guarantee that your startup ever becomes a unicorn. So, if somebody from the street answers 'No' to reverse vesting, I'll pass on him in a split second."

"Clear," I told him. "Thank you for your honesty, Steve."

"Good luck, Roman! Let's hope that Dot Love makes it. Sign a contract and we'll start."

I hung up and mumbled to myself, "Thank you, Jessica, for your big freaking mouth."

Nothing to Lose

I TOLD IGOR AND SHMAGY about my conversation with Steve and the constrained position of our balls. Shmagy shook his head and told us it was as he expected. He then retired to his room.

I think that, in addition to reverse vesting, Shmagy had grown jealous of Jessica, who preferred to spend time with rich guys from Sand Hill Road instead of him.

Igor sighed, went outside for a smoke and left without saying goodbye.

Later in the evening, I received an email from Mark, who wrote that we would have to postpone signing the contract. The hold up was my lack of employment authorization, prompting the need for Mark to discuss my situation with his immigration lawyer.

I sat alone in the kitchen and tried to make sense of everything.

I just wanted to work. I just wanted to see the woman I loved. I just wanted to live a normal life. Was that too much to ask for? It seemed like, once a weak light of hope or a drop of luck came my way, something would happen to rein me in like a horse.

On the other hand, I was in, and I had nothing to lose.

American Dream

THE NEXT DAY, I talked to Mark's immigration lawyer, Javed. He told me that Dot Love would sponsor me for a work visa, and the best people from his firm would take care of it. Later on, they would also help me to get a green card. Formally, however, I was not working for Dot Love and my shares wouldn't start vesting until my work visa was approved.

I called Mark.

"Mark," I said, "it's about reverse vesting. We just want to get past all of this with the contract and start working."

"Roman, have you talked to Javed?" he asked.

"Yes."

"So," he continued, "before you get your visa, you don't officially work, right?"

"Right. But what about five years of reverse vesting?"

"That stays," he said.

"Then we don't sign."

"What?" he responded. "Do you realize what you're doing? These are standard conditions. You have nothing yet to offer."

"What do you mean?" I exclaimed. "It was your idea to invest in Dot Love."

"I'm giving you a chance, and you are fucking it up," he said. "I do my best to help you, and you thank me by shoveling bullshit right in my face. Do you know many founders who repeated their success? There are just a few of them! The Valley knows thousands of one-time success stories. But just a few repeated ones. Would you like to know why?"

"Yes, I'd love to!" I answered.

"Because success is not only about smartness or perseverance or a brilliant idea. It's also about time, place and, mainly, luck. At this very moment, you have it all. If you say no, you also say goodbye to whatever you hoped for. It's up to you now."

"I got it, Mark. Bye."

I hung up and told my friends that I'd just buried their American dream.

A New Plan

To my surprise, the guys didn't freak out when I shared the news. Shmagy hated Hugh and was missing his steady work at NN, Inc. And Igor had had enough of all that jazz with the contract, unpaid work and fruitless hopes.

Without much interest, Shmagy asked, "So, what are we gonna do now?"

"Guys," I answered, "the conversion engine is written, right? So, the foundation is already there. Let's think of a business idea first. Then, we can add the missing features. After that, we can release and promote Dot Love ourselves. We can do it! To hell with those snakes from Sand Hill Road."

IGOR

Let's do something like a video dating site. A person registers, uploads a video presentation of himself, and those who like him can send him a message.

SHMAGY

So we'll need an internal messaging system?

ROMAN

Let's make it simple. If Person A likes a video profile of Person B and vice versa, they can see the email address of each other and can start communicating.

IGOR

But then we'll forward traffic away from our site to Gmail or whatever. The idea is that users get sucked into Dot Love.

SHMAGY

Fine! Let's enable registered users to leave comments under the video.

IGOR

But how can they communicate directly?

SHMAGY

I don't care. Just let them register and upload videos. At least that's how I see it.

IGOR

So, we are not making a dating site?

...

This continued on for another hour. In the end, we decided to write a simple messaging system or find a third-party solution.

IGOR

And how are we going to make money?

ROMAN

Let's discuss that later. If we have the WOW factor, users and money will follow.

SHMAGY

I have a cool idea. When a user comes to the page with a video profile, the video starts automatically, so the user doesn't have to press *Play*. Makes sense?

IGOR and ROMAN

Yep!

...

Then, Jessica came along and told us that, during its entire history, Silicon Valley had never seen such hopeless assheads as

Igor, Roman and Shmagy.

Oh, Ye, a Blessed Moment

IGOR STARTED DEVELOPING a new UI. As he went about his work, he printed the mockups and hung them on the kitchen walls to specify user flows.

Shmagy started coding an internal messaging system. He hated third-party solutions, "First, you trust them. Then, they do an update and fuck you up!"

I was expanding some legacy features that worked OK for a functional prototype but needed to be more robust for real-life users. For example, I added captcha to the registration page to reduce spam.

We all enjoyed our work and each other. Igor put it perfectly,

"Oh, ye, a blessed moment of creation,
A flight of thoughts,
And a myriad of hopes!
Ye tell me
If a man can ask for more."

Igor was right. It didn't feel like work. It was a narcotic, an obsession, a mighty fountain of inspiration and joy. It was a tangible feeling that Mother Fortune took our creation onto her wings and rewarded us with a true chance!

Everything was ready in two weeks. None of us remembered the last time we took showers or slept. But we did what we planned to do and even more. Dot Love was ready to meet the world.

Shmagy blessed his laptop with a cross, logged into Jenkins and pushed Dot Love to production.

What's Next?

REGARDING the first public release, startuppers are scared of two things:

1. Users ignore your site.

2. Users crash your site.

On the second count, we had no fear.

Once the release was pushed out, we did end-to-end testing on live environment and got together in the kitchen.

Then, it was for me to ask the sacred startup question, "So, what's next?"

We prepared a press release titled *Look at Our Cool Dating Site. You'll Never be Single Again* and emailed it to our friends. Those who responded said that it was a great idea, and one even registered. But no one uploaded a single video.

Shmagy took Jessica for a rowboat ride at Stow Lake in the Golden Gate Park. She made a lengthy speech on how she was looking for a soulmate who would take her to Stow Lake and ride her on a rowboat.

"Utter nonsense!" said Igor when Shmagy uploaded the video to Dot Love.

Igor and I wanted to create video profiles for ourselves. Shmagy rejected the notion, telling us that our creepy mugs would only scare users away. To be consistent, he didn't record himself either. But, alas, there was no one to scare away.

Two weeks had passed since the release, and the traffic of thirty sessions on the first day dropped to five. It looked like nobody was giving a jolly fuck about our ingenious software.

Shmagy started posting ads on Craigslist to promote Dot Love. Still, no registrations.

In desperation, he created a thousand dollar endowment and offered twenty dollars for each registration resulting in video upload. This also had no effect.

When he upped the stakes to fifty dollars, three people registered. Soon, one of them emailed us, asking us to delete her profile, as she was going to marry the next day.

Craigslist kept deleting our ads and blocking our emails for spam. Our friends praised the project, but our traffic was absurdly low.

It turned out that it's easier to write software than to attract users.

Reflections

SHMAGY had extended his unpaid leave from NN, Inc. for another month, but it was clear that he was going back once his vacation was over. Igor started to work long hours for Miss Lee as we had neglected our knife business and revenues were approaching zero.

I was out of work, and my second visitor's visa was going to expire soon. I found myself stuck, just like before. Even worse, by rejecting Mark's offer, I had screwed it up not only for myself, but also for my friends. It didn't matter that they had approved my actions at the time. Now I felt that deep inside they blamed me, knowing that our best chance to succeed was with a signed contract with Cipres Capital.

I kept adding ads for Dot Love to different sites and exchanged emails with people, but the devastating absence of any interest in our project was sucking out the last of my motivation. In the morning, I couldn't wait for the evening when I could fall asleep and forget about my failures.

Life hurts everybody, but we clench our teeth and do what we must to get back on our feet.

The real pain comes when, on top of our own

feelings of worthlessness, we harm the people we love. And that seemed to be my modus operandi since Sparrow and I had gotten drunk as pigs and been arrested by Parigin.

The Golden Gate Bridge was pulling me like a magnet. I ran there every day and stood at the same spot near the streetlight 101, waiting for something. A four-second jump into the Bay could end a sea of trouble named Roman Monin, but something inside me was refusing to give up—craving the slightest sign of hope. The Bridge pulled me like a magnet and I followed the call.

The Call

MY PHONE RANG as I stood in my usual spot on the Bridge, leaning against the streetlight 101. The caller ID was unavailable and I dropped the call, but it rang again. I answered and heard the sweetest voice in the world.

Julie was almost whispering, "Roman, my love, I only have a minute. Just tell me—do you feel the same as I do?"

"Julie!" I exclaimed. "Julie, yes, I feel it, and I think about you every day."

"That's all I needed to hear. 'Til we see each other, my love."

She hung up, and the Bridge fell down under my feet.

I reached into my backpack and took out *Martin Eden*—a book I'd become inseparable with—and opened it to the second page. There was a picture of Martin and Ruth with a quote below:

They sat idly and silently, gazing with eyes that dreamed and did not see.

A cold rain came out of nowhere, but I stood there motionless, holding my blue book open and not believing that I was awake.

Tequila

S HMAGY'S VACATION from NN, Inc was almost over, and on Friday, he decided to do one last thing for Dot Love. Just for fun, he wrote a Python script that pinged the server every second. The program would make a knock-knock sound when a new user registered and a ding-dong sound when somebody watched a video.

In the evening, Igor and Jessica showed up as always, without calling, and we began cooking dinner. Attracted by the smell of something tastier than rice and beans, hungry exchange students leaked downstairs from the third floor.

No one wanted to get drunk, but one jerk (his name was Igor) put a case of tequila on the table, and we began doing what people who had just a drop of intelligence would never do. We began to wash down tequila with beer.

Tequila is tricky. It gets to you quietly. It will not throw its power into your face before you are ready. But when you cross an invisible threshold, it drags you to places where you'd rather not be. Beer takes things to another level where tequila would never be able to climb alone.

Igor wrapped himself in bedsheets as if he was

a monk, jumped on the kitchen table, and began to preach.

"Buddha teaches us that pleasures and sufferings are illusions," he pronounced. "I agree with Buddha. But what if illusions are real? I mean, this tequila has really fucked me up!"

He dropped a shot of tequila into his beer and yelled to a Thai student who was munching on roasted chicken, "Hey, Jirapong! How do you say *Cheers* in Chinese?"

"Kanpai!" Jirapond exclaimed.

"Fuck you, too! Muahaha!" Igor yelled back and emptied his cocktail in one happy gulp.

We then remembered that we had a spinnaker line that captain Rob had given us as a keepsake after our race to Farallon Islands.

It didn't take long to stretch the line between our house and a pine tree across Fulton. Igor borrowed somebody's leather belt, oiled it with margarine, and we began zip-lining straight into the park.

When Igor, looking like a white ghost, flew over Fulton, a late dog walker saw him and screamed so desperately that somebody called the cops.

We were ready for that scenario and skulked in our house, accompanied by some hippies who had appeared out of nowhere.

Naturally, we didn't stop drinking until all the bottles in the case were empty.

Kitties

I WOKE UP on the kitchen table with my head on a pizza box.

People were making new Java programmers in each bedroom—including mine.

My stomach felt like a battle between Android and Apple fans, and each sensual "Oh!" I heard, hammered a new nail into my bleeding brain.

I was about to leave that brothel when a single ding-dong came from Shmagy's room. Then another one. Then another. Then, ding-dongs blended in a long trill.

Jessica stopped her moaning, and Shmagy crawled into the kitchen with his buzzing laptop.

"What the?" he muttered. "My program was working yesterday."

He clicked on the trackpad and there were no more ding-dongs.

"Give that to me!" I said, wincing in pain.

I made a DB query and checked the Dot Love website.

"Look!"

A user with the nickname *drunk-bird* had posted a funny video that featured two kittens playing with a ball.

The video had almost a hundred views! Almost a hundred views in the last several minutes!

Shmagy wanted to delete the video, because Dot Love was a dating site and kittens were spam. But I stopped him.

Now, it was a hundred and fifty views! And then—out of the blue—we heard knock-knock, knock-knock, knock-knock. We almost jumped. Three registrations in a minute!

"Igor!" Shmagy yelled.

A rather desperate groan came up from under the kitchen table. We pulled up our wounded comrade, nursed him with a beer, and put the laptop right into his battered face.

"Look!!"

Igor made a heroic effort to focus his eyes and asked an intelligent question that was inconsistent with his miserable state, "How did they find our site?"

I checked and discovered that Mike Scolden, the famous tech blogger, had tweeted about us.

Kittens and Technology! I love it!

He'd also provided the URL to the video with the playing kittens.

We were suddenly petrified and had no idea what to do. Then, there was another knock-knock. Then, again and again and again.

"Roman," Shmagy said, "let's post that video from the ocean race!"

"Underway!"

I uploaded the video, and we waited for a while. However, only the video with the kittens was getting views.

But WOW, the view count was approaching a thousand!

I then realized that users simply couldn't find our new video. What if we put linked thumbnails to other Dot Love videos on the right side of the video player? That thumbnail would be auto-generated, once the video was uploaded.

We decided who did what, modified the code, and committed it to GIT. I wanted to test the whole thing out on staging, but Shmagy wasn't having it.

"True cowboys don't use staging," he proclaimed as he pushed all of our changes to production.

I re-uploaded the ocean race video and checked the site. Luckily, our changes worked!

"Let's upload the *Happy birthday, bitch* video with Kevin!" Shmagy suggested.

"Mark asked me to remove it!" I objected.

"To hell with Mark!" Shmagy replied. "Look what's happening!"

That evening, we checked Dot Love stats for a day.

- 4,718 sessions

- 139 new users

- 24 user-uploaded videos

On Sunday Morning

O N SUNDAY MORNING, the Dot Love server crashed.

"Goodnight, sweet prince!" Igor exclaimed, with great joy.

We logged on to our hosting provider's site and paid for two dedicated servers.

And the madness had begun! Each day was crazier than the day before. It was our chance and nobody wanted to miss it.

Shmagy took yet another month off at NN, Inc. Igor moved to Fulton. I forgot about reflections.

Inspired by the unexpected success, we coded, tested, released and tuned things day and night.

We didn't have a long term plan, and our priorities were the availability and speed of our site. However, we did add some essential features like commenting.

It was a time when we could appreciate all of the hard work we had put into Dot Love. Our conversion engine worked like a charm, and clean code plus simple architecture allowed us to change things without worrying too much about regressions.

We kept asking each other what the business idea behind Dot Love was. Users didn't seem to want to use it as a dating site. They preferred to upload, watch and comment on homemade videos.

"Let's leave things as they are," I suggested. "Let users upload whatever they want—be it funny kittens, vomiting guys or reckless drivers."

Everybody agreed, but at the same time, we decided to check logs daily to know for sure how users were using our site. This way, we could add new features or modify or remove legacy ones.

It was a radical shift in our approach. Future functionalities were sourced not from our brains, poisoned by alcohol and other harmful substances, but rather from actual patterns of user behavior.

Let users show us the way, and we'll follow. Or not.

Hello, Again

AFTER A MONTH, we had twenty dedicated servers. It became clear that we would soon spend all our cash paying for traffic and storage. We could raise $20,000 selling Shmagy's Lexus and Igor's motorcycle. We could even max out our credit cards for another $15,000. But once it was spent, things would be over for us.

Unexpectedly, Mark called me and requested an urgent meeting.

Ever-inseparable, the three of us drove to Sand Hill Road. Shmagy tried to stay home, not wanting to deal with "the lying creep Mark and his bastard offspring Hugh." Igor tried to avoid the trip, as well, by pretending to be working on a new logo.

When we arrived, Mark flew up from the table, opening his arms for hugs.

"My dear friends," he exclaimed, "what a pleasure to see you again!"

Shmagy stepped back. So that it was Igor and I, who were tenderly embraced like two rescued puppies.

"OK, gentlemen!" he said. "Let's talk business. I'd like to revise the conditions and offer you two years of reverse vesting!"

Shmagy slowly approached the table, seating himself directly on the pile of contracts.

"Sure," Shmagy sneered, "let's talk business. No reverse vesting, no Hugh, Dot Love evaluation is 10 million, and Roman gets his green card."

"Best of luck, gentlemen!" said Mark, pointing to the door that we quickly used for our exit.

Once we merged onto 280, Mark called me and asked us to return.

In the office, we were greeted by Mark and his business partner, Steve, who had a slightly hoarse voice. They agreed to all conditions except for the evaluation of Dot Love. This, they set at 3 million.

Our trio took a minute to discuss the offer and we agreed.

The Office in Pacifica

THE NEXT MORNING, Mark emailed us a revised contract. We checked over the provisions related to our shares and found everything to be correct. I was going to take the contract to a lawyer, but we all wanted to get started quickly and just signed it. We then drove to Sand Hill Road to pass the contract to Mark and discuss further plans.

After we left Mark's office, Igor climbed on a white concrete ball and proclaimed with inspiration,

> *"When you get money*
>
> *For startup,*
>
> *Work harder, baby,*
>
> *Don't fuck up.*
>
> *For if VC withholds financing,*
>
> *You'll go straight to mama's basement."*

From there, things got rolling fast!

After only a few days, Dot Love, Inc. was officially incorporated in Delaware. Mark's lawyers opened a bank account for us and deposited a check for 900,000 dollars.

First of all, we hired Jessica as our office manager. We needed somebody to do housekeeping while we handled the programming. Her first task was to find an office for the Dot Love team, and within a week, we had moved into an old building located in the small town of Pacifica. It was right on the Pacific coast, a mere twenty minutes away from our house on Fulton.

The problem of daily bread and beer was solved by itself. As it happened, the first floor of our building was home to a pizzeria, a Cantonese restaurant and a liquor store.

The Dot Love office occupied the entire second floor—one huge room with stained, worn-out carpet and five wooden school desks. A proactive Igor brought his toolbox and connected all the desks into one long table where we could eat, work and do the other things that Shmagy and Jessica loved doing so much.

"Coiting... I mean, co-eating and co-working! That's how we roll. Right, Jess?" Igor said, looking with pride at his ugly creation.

"Jess my ass," Jessica hissed and tore out a personal desk for herself.

...

Jessica was the only person who would leave the office every evening. Igor, Shmagy and I simply moved in and used yoga mats and sleeping bags at night. Soon, Jessica would begin wrinkling her nose and complaining that our office smelled like a slum. We didn't care. Jessica called us hobos, then called a contractor and told him that there was an emergency. In a week, our office was equipped with two showers.

We couldn't imagine doing things without Jessica. She was an ideal fit for the job. She became our second mother, taking care of all the upkeep items, like food, drinks, vacuuming and even dry cleaning.

In the beginning, she looked happier than usual. Unfortunately, things would soon get worse. Shmagy kept ignoring her as a woman, still holding a grudge over her "business" connections with the rich guys. Besides, he was exhausted from working long hours. Every day, they engaged in quarrels and it was bad for the team.

We were helped by the large rat that fell from the attic and directly onto Shmagy's hairy chest as he slept on his yoga mat.

Shmagy freaked out, slapped the rat and sent it flying right into Igor's sleeping bag. Igor yelled, jumped out and made a hole in the wall with his shoulder, trying to find the exit in the darkness. The three of us would spend the rest of the night trying to catch that nippy little sucker.

Enough was enough. In the morning, we called a meeting and decreed:

1. To buy normal beds for sleeping.

2. To adopt a cat.

3. To rent an apartment nearby where Shmagy and Jessica could do whatever the heck wanted.

Shmagy volunteered for the easiest part—obtaining a cat. He visited a local shelter and found the fattest and laziest cat that he christened Basil.

Basil had a red coat and the only thing that was green about him was his lavish puke after binging on his favorite pesto pizza.

Instead of catching rats, Basil slept all day long, taking short breaks for eating, shitting and hanging with Shmagy.

"See girl, cats dig good people. Unlike you!" Shmagy was rebuking Jessica while kissing a happy Basil on his glistening forehead.

Visa

IN AMERICA, money can solve everything. But if you have the money and the connections of Mark Hortman, you can solve even more.

Mark's immigration lawyer, Javed, told me squarely that long waits were for people from the street and I, as Mark's protege, would get VIP service. He told me that the big boss wanted me to work for Dot Love and not worry about anything else. After several weeks, I received a work visa, and Javed assured me that I'd have a green card in less than a year.

Out of the dumpster, I became the CEO, Shmagy the CTO and Igor the VP of product.

Of course, we didn't forget about Jessica and granted her stock options for 0.5% of Dot Love shares.

We also negotiated an acceleration in vesting for her. This way, all of her shares would vest if Dot Love was acquired by another company. It was as good a deal as we executives had.

Check that out! We were executives!

When Jessica saw her stock options grant, she was on cloud nine—jumping, laughing, crying and hooraying all at the same time. Thanks to her previous business meetings with Kevin, Steve and other VCs, she knew that even the receptionists at Google had become millionaires when they had gone public.

Cristal Traffic

THREE MONTHS HAD PASSED since the video with funny kittens had been uploaded.

People began to talk about us in the Valley and beyond. Our crazy trinity was featured first in local, then in national news. Users, bloggers, students, Wall Street people, TV people, job seekers, social activists, even Nigerian scammers, all wanted our attention.

Just yesterday, we were nobodies. But, suddenly, thousands of people were interested in what we thought about Vladimir Putin, the NFL draft, air quality, marijuana legalization, the current price of Amazon stock and thousands of other topics that we had no idea about.

We took advantage of the situation and set up a pass to our office in the form of a bottle of elite alcohol. It was the best business idea we ever had! We soon became so spoiled that we refused to drink anything that cost less than five hundred dollars a bottle. Igor, however, left us all far behind when he got accustomed to washing his face with 2004 Louis Roederer Cristal Brut champagne.

"I cannot drink it anymore! But I also can't just look at it," Igor commented on his new habit, and we didn't judge him.

We hung a monitor on the wall with total and daily real-time stats on registered users, uploaded videos and views. All three parameters ran up like crazy.

Shmagy and I were taking care of all engineering tasks, and we both were burnt out because of the long hours, the endless responsibilities and the mounting pressure. Even Basil became stressed and started to shed his shiny red coat, as Shmagy didn't talk to him much anymore.

It was time to hire more people.

"What about Hugh?" I asked out loud and received an evil eye from everyone in the room, including Basil.

A Walk to Remember

So," I ASKED SHMAGY, "who will improve search and the list of relevant videos? Who is going to personalize stuff?"

"I can!" he said.

"No, you can't!" I objected. "You don't even have time for your best friend." I pointed to a bored Basil who sat below the stats monitor, trying to calculate a jump trajectory.

It took time to convince Shmagy, but he knew that I was right. Personalized search and relevant videos meant a real breakthrough for Dot Love, even considering our rapid growth. And Hugh had all the algorithms and even a codebase that we could integrate into the Dot Love's back end. In addition to that, Hugh had more experience than us in building distributed, scalable systems.

I received an OK from Mark and invited Hugh for a talk. To avoid any unpredictable reactions from Shmagy, I asked Hugh to meet me at the Pacifica Pier.

We walked on the beach and, the more we talked, the more I realized that Hugh was a perfect fit for Dot Love.

I shared some issues that I couldn't solve, and he came up with simple and elegant solutions without any effort. Besides, he seemed like a decent person.

"Thank God things are going smoothly," I thought to myself.

At that very moment, the ocean wave drew back and we saw an enormous Dungeness crab, crawling on the wet sand.

I didn't have a second to say, "Wow!" before Hugh rushed to catch it.

People who live outside Northern California think that the Pacific ocean is warm and peaceful. Nothing could be further from the truth. The water is ice cold, roaring waves charge the beaches like vicious dogs, and rip currents drag the best swimmers into the jaws of great white sharks.

After Hugh snatched the crab, a sleeper wave knocked him down. Another wave followed, and the poor guy was somersaulting through the water and foam like a log. And of course, he yelled, "I can't swim!"

I wasn't a stranger to doing impulsive and stupid things, so I ran to Hugh, struggling with the freezing breaker waves. We both almost drowned, trying to rescue each other. But the ocean software had a bug or, maybe, a feature and, for a minute, the waves weakened. Exhausted and scared to death, we crawled back to the beach and fell onto the warm sand.

There we lay motionless, on our backs, staring into blue skies while noisy seagulls circled above us, expecting a feast.

When Hugh's breath finally returned, he raised his right hand, and I saw the enormous Dungeness crab, caught in the death grip of his fingers.

Fucking Hugh cleared his throat and asked proudly,

"Who da man?"

Drying Up

LEANING ON EACH OTHER like two wounded soldiers, we stepped into the office and told our story to Shmagy, Igor and Jessica.

They were all laughing so hard that poor Basil hid between champagne boxes and refused to come back, even for his favorite pesto pizza.

If we were normal people, we would have been perplexed by Hugh's recklessness. But we had our own standards and his utter stupidity confirmed his eligibility for our club.

That same day, Hugh had signed a job offer for a position as Software Architect and received an option grant for 5% of Dot Love shares with acceleration in vesting.

We gave him the same low salary we paid ourselves. He had no problem with it, even though he could make four times more if he joined Apple or Google.

His sacrifice was easy to explain. Dot Love was on its way to becoming a Black Square, an ultimate WOW factor company. We had all heard rumors that some serious people from both venture funds and software companies had already approached Mark about the possible acquisition of Dot Love, or at least investing in it.

The crab also got lucky. We were about to take it down to the Cantonese restaurant for steaming when Jessica told us to steam our stupid asses first and snatched *poor crabby* away from us.

In the evening, she took Basil for their usual walk, and they released crabby straight into the wilderness of the peaceful Pacific ocean.

The Right Decision

IT TOOK US two weeks to integrate Hugh's well-written code into our codebase. We soon had a powerful, personalized search and a list of relevant videos to the right of the video player. Hugh also suggested and implemented a continuous playback feature so that the next video would start playing automatically. That way, users were lured into watching more videos, and as a result, would be spending more time on the Dot Love site.

Along with Hugh came several people, including the gifted Donald Smith.

Donald Smith could sell, loved to sell, and had to sell. He was the ideal selling machine: ZERO principles and 100% pure talent.

He would sell his own grandma if somebody offered him a dollar.

Alas, granny Smith's ideas were too wild for an unprepared world. She loved visiting our office, and her every appearance meant a disaster, be it cookies with cannabis or painting Basil pink or a MacBook Pro washed with hand soap.

It was clear where Donald had gotten his talents.

Since they were both hypnotists who used their superpowers to get laid, Donald and Shmagy became good friends. But while Shmagy was a purist and only seduced women directly, Donald preferred to pay for sex after he had closed yet another deal and received a well-deserved cut.

Donald, whose obsession with selling made him think big, set his priorities straight.

"You guys take care of your kittens and hamsters," he announced, "and I'm gonna work with large studios. I wanna turn Dot Love into the default online platform for watching TV shows and movies."

A month later, we signed a contract with the SBC network to host their classic TV show, *Greenfield*.

Then, we began talks with other studios and networks who wanted similar deals.

Then, we got sued.

Comavi Group

W<small>E KNEW</small> that some users were uploading pirated movies and even entire TV shows. Though we did our best to remove illegal content, it was impossible to check all the files.

As a result, one of the biggest entertainment networks, Comavi Group, filed a 1 billion dollar lawsuit against Dot Love for *brazen* copyright infringement.

Of course, we discussed amongst ourselves what could put Dot Love down in spite of its wild popularity. Bugs, competitors, tsunami, granny Smith, whatever—but not the lawsuit.

Mark was furious. He emailed us to say that his lawyers were on top of things and no stone would be left unturned before Dot Love was cleared of all the ridiculous charges.

I could only imagine how much Mark had to pay his lawyers, and I felt obliged to him for spending so much money to save Dot Love.

I shared my view with Donald Smith, who called me a moron for thinking that way because Mark—who wasn't a moron—would milk Dot Love for much more than he had spent on the legal fees.

One fine morning, I received an email from Comavi Group lawyers with a Cease and Desist request. They wanted us to stop the Dot Love servers and never start them again.

I called Mark, who then called his lawyers. They encouraged us to continue Dot Love's operation while they dealt with the Cease and Desist.

While waiting for Mark's call, we nearly experienced a collective heart attack. We all thought that all was over for Dot Love.

A Call from Paust

I HAD scarcely bounced back from one thing when another one came up.

Paust called me and his voice wasn't happy.

"Roman," he asked, "did you hear the news?"

"No."

"Actually," he continued, "they asked me not to tell you, but you are my best friend. And, besides..."

"Paust, stop it," I interrupted. "Just tell me."

"OK," he went on, "but, man up, bro. It's not good news..."

After a considerable pause, he told me the news.

"Julie girl has cancer. They're telling her it's not looking good. Did she call you?"

"Yes," I said, completely stunned. "But I thought it was for a different reason. Or?"

I couldn't say anything more at that moment. I felt like a cement mixer had just run over me.

"I mean, there is still hope," Paust continued. "But the doctors are asking for half a million dollars. And the only clinic that can do the surgery is in Germany."

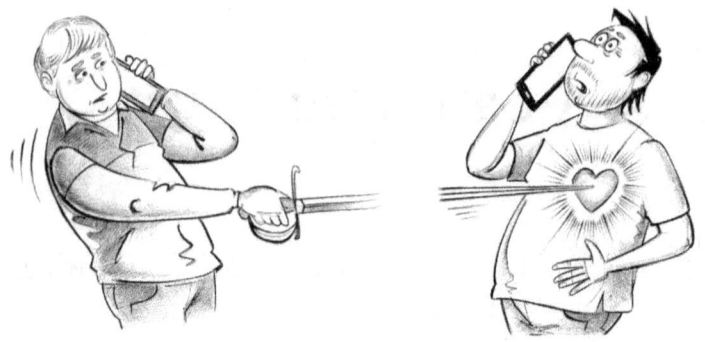

"Give me the address of the hospital," I demanded. "I'll be there tomorrow."

"Only her parents know the address."

"Then give me her parents' phone number!" I shrieked into the phone.

"I can't," he sighed. "Her parents know what happened in the subway. Parigin went out of his way to make you look like a complete deadbeat and criminal. They will not understand if I give you their number."

"So what?" I retorted. "This is about Julie. Not them, not me, not even about you."

"Sorry, man."

"OK," I replied. "I'll call you back."

I then dialed Mark.

"Mark, I must see you now."

Conversation with Mark

H I, MARK," I said, as I stepped into his office, "how much money can I get for my Dot Love shares?"

"What's going on?" he asked. "Why such a hurry?"

I told him everything. Well, not *everything*. But I explained that my woman had cancer and I needed money for her surgery.

"So, why doesn't your woman have health insurance?"

"She has," I replied. "But the surgery is not covered, and they can only do it in Germany and only for cash."

That's when Mark got rather upset with me.

"Do you now understand why I wanted five years of reverse vesting for you and your team? Thank you for proving my point. All of you former dead-beats manage to find an urgent want or need once you can put your hands on some money."

"Don't you yell at me!" I hissed back. "What do you even know about me? You'll make a fortune with Dot Love, and this is how you thank me?"

"OK, Roman," he replied. "I'll pay you 100,000 dollars for your stake."

"100,000?" I was floored. "Is that some kind of joke? My shares are worth at least 450,000. What kind of trickery is that?"

"No, it's not trickery," Mark objected. "It's just business. And I'll make sure that the board doesn't give you a single cent more. Turn your brain on now! I mean NOW! Or you'll lose your entire future—your work visa, your shares, Dot Love and our friendship."

"When can I sign the documents about the stock transfer?" I asked.

He looked at me, puzzled. Then he said, "Be here tomorrow at two."

No Longer a CEO

A FTER my unpleasant talk with Mark, I went to Fulton, where I hadn't been for at least a month.

I called Paust.

"I have one hundred thousand dollars," I told him.

"Really?" Paust replied. "Wow! Did you rob a bank?"

"Give me the address of the hospital in Germany."

"I will," he said. "Do you really love this Julie girl that much?"

"Email me as soon as you know the address."

...

I then went to the Dot Love office but was not permitted in by the new receptionist, Nora. She told me that she couldn't allow me in because of direct orders from Mark.

The next day, I picked up a check for 100,000 dollars from the Cipres Capital, and Mark's accountant asked me not to forget to pay taxes next year.

Mark saw me from his office but didn't even nod.

I endorsed the check over to Julie's name and mailed it off using the fastest option to make sure it reached the hospital in Berlin within a week.

Back at Fulton

I MOVED BACK TO FULTON and began living alone in our downstairs apartment.

When you quit a company that sponsored you for a work visa, they usually cancel your visa right away. I had no doubt that Mark would take care of that. So I accepted the idea that I was illegal, like the many people I'd known from my construction and restaurant times.

My friends—Igor, Jessica and Shmagy—would come over once in a while, supplying me with beer and the latest news. But we all felt strange. I didn't want their pity, and they didn't know how to cheer me up. In the end, we resorted to small talk while everyone tried their best to fill the uncomfortable pauses.

One day, Shmagy came alone and told me that Mark wanted to remove my name from the list of Dot Love founders. I didn't care anymore and asked Shmagy to let it go.

I had no plans for the future and lived only off my modest savings. Rice, beans and water replaced the otoro sashimi, prime rib steaks and Cristal.

I didn't care anymore.

The Irony of Fate

I SPENT several weeks in that state, calling Paust daily, only to hear, "Sorry, bro, no news."

Then, Dot Love bestowed me with a royal gift. Shmagy called to tell me.

"I just cannot believe it!" he crowed. "You are one lucky fucker!"

"Really? Since when?"

"Didn't you receive my email?" he asked.

"No."

"Shit!" he exclaimed. "Give me a minute. I forgot to press *Send*."

After a minute, I received a link to a Dot Love video. Somebody had recorded it from the same cell at the Moscow subway jail where my friend Sparrow sat as Parigin was clubbing my back with a rubber baton

At first, it focused on metal bars, then at the table. At the table, Parigin and Boris drank vodka and discussed how they had been arresting drunkards in the subway and staged assaults against each other in order to extort money in exchange for not reporting the "crime."

They even remembered me, Sparrow and Sparrow's dog, Lady.

Parigin was bragging about how smartly he had gotten rid of me, his competitor. Boris recalled the case but complained that Parigin had beaten him up worse than usual.

"Arthur," said Boris, "my face is not made of rubber, you know. But you just kept hitting me."

"No worries, Boris," Parigin replied. "It wasn't personal. I mean it was, haha! But not against you."

I forwarded the link to the video to Paust. After two hours had passed with no response, I called him. Naturally, he was outside Moscow and had no Internet access.

"Roman," he assured me, "I can watch it tomorrow."

"OK. Until tomorrow, then," I replied.

The next day, Paust called me and said that the video had been deleted. I called Shmagy. He confirmed it.

I sent an email to the user who had uploaded the video but instantly got a response with a server error, stating that the email address didn't exist. What the heck was going on?

Then, I remembered that Hugh was working on the backup system when I left Dot Love. I called him.

"Hugh," I asked, "do you have backup copies of the files uploaded in the last several days?"

"Yes, I do," he said.

"It's a question of life and death," I assured him. "I need one of the files that was deleted."

"I'm sorry, man," said Hugh. "They'll fire me if they find out. No can do."

And he hung up.

I was hating myself even more than I hated Parigin, "What an idiot I am! I should have downloaded the video and uploaded it everywhere!

I could have done just one thing right! But... But, in the end, I screwed it up like I always do."

By the absolute grace of God, Hugh called me

back.

"Ok," he said. "Give me the URL. You've saved my ass, after all."

I sent him the original URL of the deleted video. Before long, Hugh replied to me with a link to a backup copy of the file and I was able to upload it again to Dot Love.

When I had finished, I called Paust.

"Give me your father's phone number," I demanded. "NOW!"

"He is busy," Paust resisted. "Do you remember your best friend Parigin? Some cop from the General Prosecutor's office just died in his custody."

"That cop didn't die!" I roared. "Parigin killed him! I have the proof. I'm sending you an email with a link to the video right now. Forward it to Leon ASAP!"

"Aye aye, sir!"

Pepsi-Cola

After a week, Central Russian TV had a special report that included that video. Parigin and Boris the Traitor were charged with murder, extortion and abuse of authority. They were arrested, along with Parigin's father, who used his high rank to cover their crimes.

That would have never happened without Dot Love!

Leon, Paust's father, called me on Skype.

"Roman, he said, "I don't know what to say. We are all in shock here."

"Leon," I asked, "how is Julie?"

"I can only say that her surgery is scheduled."

"Is she OK?" I demanded.

"I'm sorry, Roman," he said. "I promised her father I would say nothing to anyone. When are you coming back?"

"Never."

"Really?" he asked. "Why is that?"

"What else do you expect?" I asked. "I was almost lynched in Russia. And it was America that sheltered me and gave me a second chance. Isn't it logical that I would want to live in America and not Russia? I'm grateful to you for letting me flee, but you are a part of a system that treats humans like garbage."

"OK, I gotcha," he said. "Come back when you are tired of Pepsi-Cola."

A Prodigal Bro

S HMAGY moved back to Fulton the same day.

"I'm tired of that shit," he said, pouring us Cristal. "I'm back. Embrace your prodigal bro."

I asked him to explain himself. He told me that the situation with the lawsuit was getting uglier every day.

Someone ran software automation around the clock to register new accounts and upload video files containing movies and TV shows that belonged to Comavi Group.

An internal investigation, led by Shmagy, came to a sad conclusion. Whoever tried to screw Dot Love knew what he was doing.

Each illegal upload was unique because the same content was concealed with some minor change in the wording of the title or video file itself: the filename, file size, or file format would be slightly different.

The attackers also kept changing their IP addresses.

Neither our copyright detection system nor Dot Love employees could single out and delete illegal content as quickly as it was uploaded.

On the other hand, illegal content was just a tiny drop in a flood of legitimate videos, and the stats indicated a rapid growth in user base, views and uploads.

When Shmagy finished, I had to go outside, as I didn't want him to see my wet eyes. Dot Love was my baby and it hurt like hell to realize that I had become nobody in the very company I had founded.

Relentless Comavi Group

ONE FINE DAY, fourteen Dot Lovers, almost the entire team, poured into our Fulton apartment. They told me that Mark, accompanied by security guards and police, had paid them a visit during their lunch break. Mark had produced a court order, and everyone had been escorted out of the building—except Hugh, who had been helping Mark, and Basil, who had been sleeping on the stats monitor.

"We have no idea what to do!" shouted Nora, the receptionist. "Roman, tell us what to do!" She was sobbing on Shmagy's shoulder.

Everyone began talking, calling, posting and texting until Shmagy's phone rang. He yelled, "Shut up, everybody! It's Mark."

Shmagy turned on the speakerphone.

"Shmagy," Mark began, "things got out of hand and I owe you an explanation."

"Mark, what the fuck?" puzzled Shmagy.

"Comavi Group won," Mark replied. "A judge decided to stop all our servers. It's all done."

"And what now?"

"Now," continued Mark, "you are all laid off. Why should I pay you a salary if the site is dead?"

"What do you mean *dead*?" Shmagy objected. "We can appeal! Your lawyers are on it."

"Not any longer," Mark replied. "I had to sell Dot Love to cover my losses."

"What? How? You couldn't!"

"I could and I had to. By the way, hello everybody!" Mark sneered.

"Die, you bitch!"

Shmagy's Nokia flew into the wall and broke into a thousand pieces.

"That's it, gang," he said. "Go home."

Without Dot Love

L AID OFF Dot Lovers had to sign an agreement that they held no claims against Dot Love, Mark Hortman or Cipres Capital. They also had to consent to not working for companies dealing with videos or social networks for the next five years.

Only after signing the agreement could they get their final paychecks—three months' salary.

Dot Love co-founders, Igor and Shmagy, didn't make a cent out of their Dot Love shares, to say nothing of all laid-off employees.

Had we read the entire 200-page contract in the first place, we would have known that Cipres Capital would receive a special kind of stock—*participating preferred*. That meant that, in case of liquidation, they would get their initial investment back as a minimum.

We were lambs, first attacked by the Comavi Group, and then slaughtered by our own shepherd.

Shmagy never returned to NN, Inc. and was spending his savings on drinking and fucking around.

Igor had simply disappeared.

I also wanted to leave Fulton and never return.

The Cipres Capital Strikes Back

THE APARTMENT was empty. Shmagy was chilling in Carmel with his new girlfriend. After the fiasco with Dot Love, Jessica left him or, more precisely, all of us.

I put Martin Eden into the backpack, left the door keys on the kitchen table, and stepped outside.

"So long. Be well," I said to the house and started towards Geary boulevard.

A car beeped behind me. I turned my head and saw none other than Kevin! At the wheel of his McLaren!

The man and his iron horse looked like a living poster of *Life Is a Success*.

"Hey, stranger!" he called. "I've heard you are in trouble? Need a ride?"

"Kevin!" I exclaimed. "Wow! How are you? I'm sorry I never visited you in the hospital."

"It's OK. Hop in!"

I hopped into the car. The engine roared, the McLaren yanked forward and we nearly started spinning like we did in our accident on Sand Hill Road.

"You don't look so bad after a coma," I told him.

"I never was in a coma."

"Where have you been then?" I asked.

"In Hawaii!" he chirped. "By the way, you almost blew my cover with your video. I've become a freaking Internet meme. When people see me, they say *Happy Birthday, bitch!*"

"Wait! Where?"

"In Hawaii!" he replied. "Swimming, fucking, drinking and sometimes consulting the FBI on interesting financial topics. For example, how a dirtbag like Mark Hortman fucked you up over Dot Love. It was his idea with Comavi Group. It all was a setup. And his sweet boy, Hugh, was a mole. How else do you think they knew how to pass your copyright detection?"

"Pull over, man!" I exclaimed. "But why did they do it?"

"To own Dot Love, of course!" replied Kevin. "You can sell it for 30 million now, but Mark sold it to his own company for 1 dollar. Not only did he fuck you, but also Cipres Capital. That's why he plotted all that pressure from Comavi Group."

"So, there was no team of lawyers?"

"Of course not!" Kevin laughed. "It all was a show. I bet you know his favorite line: *All the world's a stage, and all the men and women merely players!* By the way, when was the last time you visited the Dot Love website?"

"I don't remember," I said. "I thought the site was dead."

"Oh, no!" Kevin replied. "It's alive and kicking!

"The court order was appealed immediately, and the day after they threw out the Dot Love team, a new team was working in the Pacifica office with Hugh as their CEO. The site is up and the traffic is so heavy that CPUs are sparkling and smoking."

"But why didn't the FBI arrest Mark and Hugh?" I asked him.

"They just did. And I came straight to you!"

"So what's gonna happen?" I wondered aloud.

"The Pacifica office is sealed now, but I'm working with the government to acknowledge the Dot Love sale as null and void. Once it's done, all Dot

Love shareholders will get their stocks back, and the old team can return to the office. So, get ready, mister CEO."

"I'm not a CEO," I said. "I sold my Dot Love stake and lost my work visa. It's all over for me."

"Well, I haven't seen any papers," Kevin said as he winked. "Formally, you are a CEO. And $100,000 is your performance bonus from Cipres Capital. Here is your check, by the way. We got it from Germany."

"But I sold my shares!"

"No, Roman," he said. "Is this your life's principle? Not reading contracts?"

"So, I'm in?!"

"Of course! Cipres Capital is betting on you. But first, you need to take care of something else."

Kevin drove me to Lincoln Boulevard and pointed to the Golden Gate Bridge.

"Go now," he said. "Someone is waiting for you."

At First Sight

I FELL IN LOVE WITH ROMAN *at first sight. I taught the class that day, and he was looking at me with such tenderness and awe that I could hardly concentrate. He didn't show up often at the Law School, but every time I saw him, I found myself at a loss for words. Fortunately, Vlad Paustovsky, my childhood friend, was his friend too. The informal meeting I had dreamt about happened the same day as the exam on the History of Modern Capitalism.*

When Professor Victoria called me, I jumped for joy! Roman was always bugging her, asking why lawyers had to study her course instead of more practical things, like civil law. Professor Victoria had a beef against Roman, and he had no chance of passing the exam, even if he was prepared. It meant his expulsion from the Law School and two years away in the army—and that I couldn't allow.

When they told me about the situation in the subway, I was sure that Roman was innocent, even though I didn't know him very well. I did know Parigin very well. For many years, he had poisoned my life, using any opportunity, including our parents' friendship, to get closer to me. I lost count of all the nasty things he did. But our parents didn't worry about him stalking me, saying that it was normal for a boy to court a girl.

I asked Leon Paustovsky to investigate the case properly, but he didn't want to listen to me and promised to put Alex "The Sparrow" in the cage if Roman ever called me or returned. I knew that Leon would do that because he cared, but he had no idea how tired I was of other people deciding what was right for me.

When Roman left Moscow, I got in touch with Sparrow. We started to call each other. Along with my friend, Helen, we visited him and his dog, Lady, several times. Sparrow told me a lot about Roman, and I fell deeper in love. To my joy, Helen and Sparrow began to date. They are a great match: both are quiet, kind and soft, and both love animals.

Vlad the "Paust," who was probably frightened by his father, was reluctant to talk to me. We almost lost contact.

The first months were the hardest as I had no info about Roman while Parigin kept showing up, promising to **deal** with him. I told that to my parents, but they didn't take it seriously. The main thing they cared about was my Ph.D. and the image of the good girl from a good Moscow family. I felt like a prisoner.

Then something terrible happened to me. I went to the hospital with severe pneumonia. The doctors conducted an X-ray and saw something scary, so they wanted to do some tests. One day, a doctor, along with my parents, came to my hospital room and told us that I, who had never smoked a single cigarette, had lung cancer.

It's better not to remember what happened to my parents when they heard the news. They looked as if some unseen force had sucked away all their joy and desire to live. They tried to smile and cheer me up, but it was me who had to smile and cheer them up. Their pain was indescribable.

I managed to get Roman's phone number and called him. I had to hear his voice. And, when I did, I knew that the many months of separation had only strengthened our love. I needed to hear his voice to be able to fight the disease and to know that he, my most beloved and desired, felt what I felt: the unbreakable connection of our hearts.

I hesitated before the call, but then I realized that if something as bad as this had happened to him, he would want to receive the first phone call from me and have me as the last person he ever saw. We didn't need to pity each other. We had to keep our love until the end.

I couldn't talk for long because a heavy cough could flare up, but even a minute was enough.

It was Sparrow who told me about Dot Love's press release and that nobody was interested in Roman's project. Helen, Sparrow and I held a Skype conference to discuss how we could help

Roman promote Dot Love. I could ask my friends and colleagues to create video profiles, but that didn't seem like a good idea.

During the video call, two kittens that Hellen and Sparrow had recently adopted, were jumping and playing, and we all were laughing at their mischief. I asked if Sparrow had videos of them and he said, "Probably a gigabyte."

Then Helen had an ingenious idea. Several years ago, there had been an exchange student from America. His name was Mike Scolden. He didn't become a legal scholar but managed to start a wildly popular tech blog. I emailed him. He replied in no time, saying that he had the best memories about Russia and our Law School. Then, we had a great talk on Skype, catching up on all sorts of things. At one point, he asked me if there was something he could do for me, for the sake of good old times.

I told him Roman's story. He confirmed that he had heard something about Dot Love, but had no idea about the **eventful life** of its founder.

"You know, Julie, here is an idea: upload a catchy video and send me a link. I'll be happy to tweet it," Mike offered.

Sparrow, Helen and I spent the whole weekend watching a gigabyte of kitten videos. In the end, we found the funniest one.

Sparrow registered as **drunk-bird** and uploaded the video to Dot Love. I emailed the link to

Mike, and he made that famous tweet that turned things around.

I was happy and proud that we could help Roman. Unfortunately, my health was getting worse. My parents grew disappointed with my doctors and started to look for a hospital abroad. Naturally, all of our friends, including the Parigins and the Paustovskys, found out about my cancer.

Parigin arrived at the hospital with a bouquet of red roses and promised me his eternal love and inexhaustible riches. But when he saw blood on the towel following one of my violent coughing fits, he freaked out and left.

Parigin's mother called me, asking me to take care of her poor baby. After seeing blood on the towel, he completely lost it and killed the family dog. I couldn't keep myself together and called her an idiot. When I told my father about the conversation, he called the Parigins and told them that their "poor baby" would spend the rest of his short life in an intensive care unit if he ever bothered me again.

Leon Paustovsky helped us find a hospital in Germany where they accepted and sometimes cured hopeless patients like myself. I went to Berlin for a health examination. The surgery would cost us 600,000 dollars, and my father put our Moscow apartment and country house up for sale.

Then, they brought me a check from Cipres Capital for 100,000 dollars. It was from Roman, endorsed to my name. I showed the check to my father. He hugged me and we both started to weep. I asked him to mail the check back. I had a feeling that Roman had gotten himself into trouble trying to help me.

Several days after I received the check, my German doctor entered my hospital room with a shining smile on his face. He told us that I was misdiagnosed and had never had cancer. They would be able to care for my complications caused by the pneumonia, and considering the new diagnosis, the price tag would be much lower.

By that time, my family was so frustrated and exhausted that we decided to keep my new diagnosis to ourselves.

My doctors changed the course of treatment. Soon, I began to feel better. Everyone was surprised by my speedy recovery, but I wasn't. I had someone I loved and a chance to live. What else could one ask for? I felt such an upsurge of hope that my health started coming back to me, not by the day, but by the hour.

Then, they arrested Parigin, his father and his accomplice, Boris. There was a big scandal, especially considering Parigin's father position in the government.

I called Roman, but he didn't pick up. I emailed him, but he didn't reply. His Skype was offline and he didn't see my messages.

I got in touch with Mike Scolden, and he confessed that he had told Roman's story to Kevin.

Kevin soon called me and said—off the record— that he was 'officially' in a coma but 'unofficially' in Hawaii. He told me that he'd love to arrange a big surprise for Roman if I could come to San Francisco ASAP.

Kevin couldn't see my packed suitcase with an envelope on it. I opened the envelope, put a flight ticket to San Francisco into my pocket, and called a taxi to the airport.

On the Bridge

SHE STOOD at my spot near the streetlight 101. The wind was playing with her hair, and the sun was trying to kiss her through shreds of fog.

We rushed towards each other. I caught Julie and hugged her.

"Here I am, my love," she whispered.

We did not ease off our embrace, as if we were afraid of awakening. But when we realized that it was not a dream, we looked at each other and drowned in a kiss. We were shaking with happiness, desire and an amazing feeling of freedom, as if we had found what was ours, and no one could take it from us.

"Here I am, my love," she said again.

The fresh wind came flying from the Farallon Islands and dispersed the fog.

The rays of the setting sun splashed fire on San Francisco, and it sparkled under the blue sky.

I took Martin Eden from my backpack, opened the book to the second page and showed Julie a picture of Martin and Ruth.

"Julie, look!" I exclaimed.

We hugged again, and the book slipped from my hands.

But no one moved.

We...

We

stood

idly

and

silently,

gazing

with eyes

that dreamed

and

did not see.

Epilogue

GOD BLESS SAN FRANCISCO!

Bless its green parks and busy streets, its orange and sometimes crimson Bridge, its mischievous dwellers, its freezing fogs and especially, its gentle and rare sun. Bless the coarse sand of Baker Beach, the steaming cauldrons on Pier 39, the decadence of Height and the bustle of Chinatown. And bless all of us, the dreamers who have dropped from the clouds on its steep hills, believing in our Chance.

Life can beat us, and cold rains can pierce through our shelter, but we will go on because we love the City, and in return, it will always give us our Chance.

That is the deal.

So it was.

So it is.

So it will be.

THE BEGINNING

AUTHOR

Roman Savin

ARTIST

Sergei Korsun

ARTIST ("MEETING ON THE BRIDGE")

Tanya Tkacheva

EDITOR

Pamela Hennessy

PROOFREADER

Amy Paschal

Konstantin Latysh

Maximilian Latysh

COVER

Juan Francisco Garrido

LAYOUT

Roman Savin

WWW.QATUTOR.COM